LAWMAN'S WITNESS

B.J. DANIELS

INTRIGUE

This one is for Scott McMillion, who read my very first book, reviewed it and still has it on his bookshelf. You're a good friend, Scott. Thanks for your support all these years. Check out Scott's *Montana Quarterly Magazine* for wonderful photos, articles and stories about the state we love to write about.

Recycling programs for this product may not exist in your area.

ISBN-13: 978-1-335-69072-2

Lawman's Witness

Harlequin Enterprises ULC
22 Adelaide St. West, 41st Floor
Toronto, Ontario M5H 4E3, Canada
www.Harlequin.com

HarperCollins Publishers
Macken House, 39/40 Mayor Street Upper,
Dublin 1, D01 C9W8, Ireland
www.HarperCollins.com

Printed in Lithuania

1 2 3 4 5 6 7 8 9 10 LIT 28 27 26 25

"I'm getting a lot of pressure from the higher-ups to stop investigating."

"You could lose your job?"

"I'm more worried about letting you down or failing to keep you from getting killed."

Amy Sue sat back and took a breath. "I'm just afraid that no matter what I do, Jack Marshall is going to get away with murder. I suspect you are worried about that, too, Detective."

He laughed. "Isn't it time you called me Russ?"

"Russ." She liked the sound of it on her lips and felt heat rush to her center as their gazes met. His eyes were a rich warm brown like melted dark chocolate, his lashes long. It struck her how handsome he was, especially when he smiled.

But it was the look in those eyes that sent butterflies flitting around in her chest. Like a lightning bolt, she felt the electricity of it spiking not just desire, but an aching need she'd never felt so strongly before.

Russ's look promised so much more than she'd ever dreamed possible.

New York Times and *USA TODAY* bestselling author **B.J. Daniels** lives in Montana with her husband, Parker, and three springer spaniels. When not writing, she quilts, boats and plays tennis. Contact her at bjdaniels.com, on Facebook or on X @bjdanielsauthor.

Also by B.J. Daniels

Harlequin Intrigue

Renegade Wife

Dry Gulch, Montana

Reckoning with the Cowboy
Targeting the Sheriff
Lawman's Witness

Silver Stars of Montana

Big Sky Deception
Missing: Baby Doe
Engaging the Deputy

Canary Street Press

Powder River

Dark Side of the River
River Strong
River Justice

Visit the Author Profile page at Harlequin.com.

CAST OF CHARACTERS

Russell Tate—There is no body, no evidence and the alleged killer was out of town that night. So why does he believe the eyewitness against all odds?

Amy Sue Brand—The eyewitness swears she saw a murder and recognized the killer. If she's wrong, why is he now after her?

Jack Marshall—The prominent car dealer was bulletproof—until he picked up the wrong young woman hitchhiker.

Christine Marshall—She'd give up her privileged lifestyle over her dead body.

Whitney Clark—All she wants is a wealthy man who can make her dreams come true—even if she has to blackmail him.

Liz Baker—She feared her former roommate was dead. But getting justice could kill her.

Chapter One

As he sharpened the knife, he found himself humming an old song. Something about all the ways to leave a lover. He'd left a lot of lovers. An expensive bangle or cold, hard cash often did the trick to smooth over his exit so he could walk away clean.

What he didn't like was one that gave him trouble. The few that had put up an argument had gotten to see the ugly side of him he worked to keep hidden. After glimpsing the less charming side of him, they were smart enough to realize the affair was over and graciously accept his goodbye gift, glad to disappear from his life and not look back.

But this latest one… He shook his head. He hadn't expected her to be a problem. She was young, a student, a free spirit. Unfortunately, she, too, had a hidden part of her that when it came out wasn't just ugly, it was dangerous. She'd fooled him and would now make more than a fool out of him if he didn't stop her. This one had turned treacherous with her threats and her desperation. No, this one wasn't going away quietly.

He gently touched the pad of his thumb to the knife and felt the bite of the blade as he remembered the gleam in her eyes when she told him all the ways she would destroy him and the life he'd built. His fingers began to ache as he gripped the knife handle harder at the memory. He had tried to warn her where her threats would get her, but she wouldn't listen. He would either divorce his wife and marry her or she would bury him.

She'd given him no choice. He told her he would make her dreams come true when they met tonight. He couldn't wait for the moment when she realized she'd set her sights on the wrong man.

As he carefully wrapped the knife in a cloth and put it in his briefcase, he couldn't get that darned tune out of his head. This time, there was only one way to leave his lover.

Amy Sue Brand was lost, because this couldn't be the place she'd rented. She fought back the sense of panic that threatened to overwhelm her as she tried to see into the pitch blackness. "This is what happened when a Montana girl right off the farm goes to the big city," she said, her voice cracking a little inside her SUV as she made another pass through the cul-de-sac. Her headlights revealed the skeletons of houses still under construction before she reached the address she'd been given.

"This can't be it," she said, not for the first time. Yet this was definitely the address she had on her phone along with the code for the door in the back. Why hadn't she just gone to a hotel? Because she'd gotten a good deal online for a small apartment for the week.

The building was narrow, two stories high, and it did look as if the construction might have been completed. She checked the address again on her phone; maybe she wasn't wrong. Maybe this was it. She just hadn't expected it to be so far from Billings or so spooky out here with few to no lights.

Low clouds hung over the city like a wet blanket suffocating any light. Out here miles away there was only blackness and no sign of people anywhere near. The stark outlines of unfinished structures rose out of the night like ghosts in what appeared to be a new subdivision.

If only she'd gotten here in the daylight. She'd been held up first with road construction and then by a semi rollover that blocked both lanes of the two-lane highway. If that hadn't made her late enough, she'd gotten caught in a cattle drive not far out of Dry Gulch. A father and son had been moving the herd down the middle of the road.

Now the night was black; she was tired and felt completely turned around. She looked at the narrow, tall building in her headlights. This was the short-term rental apartment she'd booked? All the windows were dark. Was the place even finished? Maybe.

A gust of wind rocked her SUV, cold blowing through the cracks around her car door. She wouldn't be surprised to wake up to snow in the morning. At twenty-eight, she'd seen it snow every month in Montana one year or another, she thought, instead of thinking she might have been scammed by the nice-sounding young man who'd rented her the place sight unseen. He'd required cash for the full week up front, which she'd sent him.

Remembering his directions, she pulled alongside the narrow building, driving through the deep shadow to the back. "Don't let this be a scam," she said under her breath as she imagined what her sister would have to say about this.

Her headlights shone on a huge pile of dirt directly behind the unit where she was told she would find the back door. Determined to see this through, she grabbed her purse and, shoving open her door with effort against the wind, stepped out into the night.

Shivering from the cold, she moved to the rear of the SUV and opened the hatch to get her suitcase and winter coat. It was too cold and windy to make two trips, so she had to trust this was the right place as she made her way along the dark side of the building next to her vehicle.

The young man had told her that there was a light by the back door, so all she had to do was key in the code he'd given her and she'd be all set.

As she turned the corner of the building, she found it much darker back here. She could barely make out the outline of the house right next door. Why had she dropped her phone into her purse? She was going to need the flashlight to even find the door, let alone the keypad to put in the code.

With a growing sense of dread, she couldn't shake the feeling that she'd been scammed and was now wasting time. She should just go to a hotel. But if this was the apartment she'd seen online…

As she dug blindly in her large, deep purse for her phone, she moved cautiously along the back of the building. "Just get this over with," she whispered to herself. Yep, her sister Josie would have a whole lot to say about this. Which was exactly why she hadn't told Josie about the cute little apartment she'd rented instead of staying at the hotel with the rest of the workshop attendees. At least the photos the man had sent her had been of the inside of a cute little apartment.

Her ears pricked up for a moment. Was that the sound of a car she'd heard over the wind? She moved quicker, feeling her way along the back wall. She'd just found a slightly recessed doorway and was still groping for her phone when she was startled by the sound of car doors slamming and a vehicle engine as one car left.

Someone was here. She froze for an instant before she heard voices, a man's and a woman's muffled by the window. A few seconds later she caught movement as the two passed by to go to the back of the house next door. A light came on inside the house.

With a flood of relief, Amy Sue realized that she wasn't completely alone out here. Though she couldn't imagine that the house was occupied. As lights came on upstairs, she saw that she was right. The entire house was still under construction. She could see the bare studs of an unfinished wall and plastic hanging from a doorway as a woman stepped into view, a man right behind her. With a shock she saw that the woman had a blindfold over her eyes. Both were dressed in semiformal attire as if headed out to dinner.

From where Amy Sue stood in the darkness behind the small apartment building, she saw the man move the plastic aside as he urged the blindfolded woman deeper into the house. The woman, who'd appeared excited at first, now seemed reluctant to go any farther into the construction area. She was trying to untie the covering on her eyes, but the man seemed equally determined to stop her.

While Amy Sue couldn't see the man's face, she could see his hands pulling hers away from the blindfold. The woman shook her head adamantly and struggled to push past him back the way they'd come in.

Spellbound by what she was seeing, Amy Sue hadn't moved, had hardly taken a breath. She saw the man grab the woman roughly as she tore off the blindfold. He had his arms around her as if trying to restrain her from leaving. It all seemed to happen in seconds, Amy Sue's horror growing as she watched them locked in a battle of wills.

But just as quickly as it had started, the woman stopped struggling and slumped against her date. As she did, he jerked the construction plastic from the doorway, wrapping it around her as he began to lower her body to the floor.

Amy Sue stared in shock at the bright red stain on the man's white dress shirt and the blood-stained knife in his hand. Her held breath expelled in a gasp as she realized what she'd just witnessed.

She stumbled back, bumping into the rear wall of the building. As she reached out to steady herself, she activated the light by the door she hadn't been able to find earlier. Now standing in a blinding puddle of gold, her gaze flew to the house next door to see the man framed in the window looking directly at her.

As their gazes met, she felt stunned.

She recognized him.

For an instant, her feet refused to move. Her fingers opened, dropping her suitcase. She turned, running back the way she'd come only to crash into the front of her SUV as it appeared out of the darkness. Limping, she worked her way around to the driver's side in terror that she would hear his footfalls on the path behind her.

Hands shaking, she unlocked the driver's-side door,

yanking it open and throwing herself into the seat behind the wheel. As she grabbed the door handle and slammed it shut, she frantically reached to start the engine, the doors locking as the engine roared.

She realized her phone was still in the bottom of her purse, but she didn't dare take the time to find it. Slamming the SUV into gear, she glanced out into the darkness, terrified that she would see the man running toward her with the knife in his hand.

As she hit the gas, the vehicle jumped forward, startling her to realize that she'd accidently put the car into Drive in her panic. She managed to slam on the brakes before the SUV crashed into the pile of dirt illuminated in her headlights.

Fingers trembling, she threw the vehicle into Reverse and sped backward, flying past the side of the building and coming to a stop at an odd angle in the middle of the cul-de-sac. When she looked up, she saw him.

He was standing on the second story balcony of the house where he'd murdered the woman. She stared at him for a moment, confused. He hadn't come after her? Why was he just standing there so calmly watching her? Didn't he realize she was going to the police to tell them what she'd seen?

She shuddered, chilled at the sight of him as she slammed the car into Drive and hit the gas. As she sped off, she looked back and saw that the balcony was empty.

He was coming after her now.

Her whole body shook even as her mind tried to make sense of what she'd seen. Gripping the wheel and fighting the urge to drive too fast, she kept watching her rearview mirror expecting to see the man's headlights suddenly appear behind her as she drove toward the lights of the city. She didn't pull over until she reached a well-lit busy gas station. Digging her phone out of her purse, she called 911.

"I just saw a murder!"

Chapter Two

Amy Sue couldn't remember the last time she'd ugly-cried. But just the sight of her sister coming through the door of the police station made her burst into tears.

Josie rushed to her and quickly wrapped her in her arms, patting her back with one hand and pulling a tissue from her purse with the other. Her sister, the lawyer, was always prepared for tears, though not normally from Amy Sue.

Josie was always prepared for most things because she was like their grandmother. She had some version of second sight that meant she sensed things before they happened. But after a recent fall and head injury she'd said the "knowing" was gone. Which might be true since Josie certainly hadn't seen this coming any more than Amy Sue had.

"Glad you're here," the nicer of the two detectives, Russell Tate, said to Josie once the four of them were seated in the interrogation room, a cup of bad coffee in front of each of them. Amy Sue had noticed how differently he dressed from the other detective. Detective Tate wore a Western shirt, jeans and freshly polished boots. She'd seen the Stetson hanging by his desk when she'd come in half out of her mind trying to get someone to help her.

She'd liked Detective Tate better than the other detective right away. An attractive man with a full head of curly brown hair and warm brown eyes, he was closer to her own age. When he looked at her it was with kindness rather than suspicion. She didn't have her sister's second sight, but studying him and his sun-browned hands, she knew he would be good with horses.

That her mind had gone that route made her even more sure that she'd lost her mind tonight.

"She *claims* she witnessed a murder," the other detective, Curtis Hanson, said to her lawyer sister, leaning heavily on the word *claims*. Short and stocky with what appeared to be a permanent frown, Curtis Hanson was older than his partner by at least ten years. He was dressed in a suit, the tie loose, the jacket wrinkled and smelling like the spearmint breath mint he'd popped in his mouth. He made Amy Sue nervous as she watched him weave his pen through his fingers restlessly as he studied her from across the table.

With her adrenaline waning, Amy Sue felt wrung out. She'd been here all night, she'd told her story repeatedly and, to her exasperation, hadn't been believed.

"I know what I saw," she said for the hundredth time. "He killed her right in front of me." From the moment she'd walked into the station, the police had been skeptical after she'd told them that she'd recognized the killer. "I saw Jack Marshall stab the woman, then grab the plastic sheeting hanging from the doorway to wrap it around her body as he lowered her to the floor. When he stood up, his shirt was soaked with blood. That's when he looked out the window. I recognized him and stumbled back, bumping into the wall behind me. An outside light came on and he looked right at me."

"Jack Marshall? The man from the car ads?" her sister asked, sounding as astonished as the cops had been.

"I know what I saw," Amy Sue snapped.

From the chair next to her, Josie reached over to take her hand, squeezing it gently. "I'm sorry. I wasn't questioning what you saw. I was just surprised like the police are that it was him."

"One of our most prominent citizens," Hanson said. "He owns the largest car dealership in the state. He and his wife are very active, donating thousands of dollars a year to local charities. They're also active in politics, host the governor when he's in town."

"Thank you, Detective," Josie said. "We get the picture."

"It was him," Amy Sue cried. "I recognized him right away. I've seen his inane ads on TV enough over the years. It was Jack Marshall. He looked right at me."

"You say he definitely saw you?" her sister asked, concern edging her voice.

"*He saw me*. He saw my car and since he owns a car dealership, he'd know the make and model even if he didn't get my license plate number when he watched me leaving."

Hanson made a disbelieving sound. "Leaving the scene of what you thought was a murder. Dropping your suitcase and running? Why not just call the police?"

"I'd witnessed a murder," she said, unable to hide her exasperation. "I wanted to get out of there as quickly as possible. I was afraid to take the time to dig my phone from my purse to call the police until I'd gotten away." She saw Hanson exchange a look with her sister before he spoke directly to Josie.

"When we arrived at the house, we found no sign of an altercation, no sign of a murder and no body." Hanson shook his head, still twirling the pen. "No blood, no nothing. No sign that anyone had even been there. Also, there were no sheets of plastic like your sister described." He raised his hand without looking at Amy Sue as he quickly added, "We called the general contractor. He said he'd ordered the plastic on the floors and doorways removed *yesterday morning* because the Sheetrock guys are coming Monday."

Amy shook her head. "That can't be right," she said, trying not to raise her voice. "I saw him grab the plastic sheeting from the doorway before he put down her body. There must have still been plastic on the floor as well. It explains why he didn't seem in a hurry to cover up his crime. He must have known that he had plenty of time to get away before I could report it and you could get out to the house. With all the plastic around, of course there wasn't any blood or evidence of the murder."

"Sounds like you have it all figured out," Detective Hanson said. "So, who was the woman he allegedly killed?"

Amy Sue started to speak, but her sister squeezed her hand to stop her. "I believe that's your job," Josie said. "My sister has already told you she didn't recognize the young blonde woman. She's explained what she witnessed, and you've taken her statement. Have you been able to reach Jack Marshall?"

"He's out of town," Detective Hanson said, sounding

pleased at the news. "He's been gone all weekend," he added, as if daring Amy Sue to argue the point.

"According to whom?" her sister inquired.

"His wife," Detective Tate, the cowboy cop, said.

Josie sat back and let go of Amy Sue's hand. "Yes, the wife is always the last to know, isn't she."

The detective dropped the pen. "I don't know what you're insinuating."

"Of course you do," Josie said. "My sister has told you in her statement sitting in front of you exactly what she saw. They appeared to be a couple. He was showing her the house, which would explain her excitement—until he killed her. It is perfectly clear that my sister witnessed a murder and got a good look at the killer. Now do your job."

"What was your sister even doing there in the first place?" Hanson demanded. "That apartment she said she'd rented wasn't finished, let alone available to rent. We talked to the owner of the property. He didn't rent it to her."

"It doesn't matter what she was doing there. She rented the place online and was clearly scammed since as you say, the apartment isn't finished. Her accidentally being there has nothing to do with what she witnessed. I'm sure the killer picked that spot because he thought no one would be there," Josie said in her calm lawyer voice. "Clearly someone took advantage of her online. Unless you're interested in tracking down the person to get her money back… I didn't think so. My sister saw Jack Marshall kill a woman. I don't know how he did it, but you can bet he did."

Hanson sighed. "Look, I don't know what your sister

thought she saw, but she didn't see Jack Marshall. Jack has an airtight alibi. He was at a conference in Great Falls all weekend and isn't expected back until tomorrow." The detective glanced at his phone screen. "Make that today, since it is now Sunday. Business associates at the convention will verify that he was there."

"But you haven't talked to all of them, have you?" Josie shook her head. "How convenient he was out of town, yet you have an *eyewitness* who says he was not in Great Falls at a conference but here in Billings stabbing a woman to death. You also have a time of death because my sister saw the whole thing."

"Right," the detective said. "But what we don't have is a murder victim."

"Yet," Josie said, and rose from her chair. "We're finished here."

Rising as well, Amy Sue looked at the two detectives, Hanson with his suspicions and Tate with his sympathy, which was almost worse. She felt sick to her stomach after what she'd witnessed. But the real horror was that they didn't believe her, making her wonder if she could have been wrong. If Jack Marshall was in Great Falls all weekend, then how could she have seen him? Exhaustion, confusion and her waning adrenaline had her fighting tears as she followed her sister out of the interrogation room.

"What if I'm wrong?" she said to Josie as they left the police station. "What if I only thought it was him?"

Her sister stopped walking to look at her. "I know you. If you said you saw Jack Marshall kill that woman, then that's who you saw. It's up to the detectives to find out how he did it."

"They won't, though!" she cried. "They don't believe me."

"But I do," Josie said.

Amy Sue felt overwhelmed to have her sister on her side. "What would I do without you?"

"You're never going to have to find out," Josie said, and took her arm as they walked toward their vehicles in the lot. The sun broke free of the horizon to the east, promising a new beautiful Montana cloudless day. "Let's take your SUV. I want to see where this happened."

Glad for the warmth of the sun, it was still blinding as Amy Sue handed her sister the keys. "You drive. I can't right now. The route is still in the navigation system."

Josie looked over at her in concern. "If you'd rather not go back there—"

"I'm okay, just still upset. They don't even believe that I was scammed when I rented the apartment next door. Doesn't it bother you that these things always happen to me?"

"You're kind and trusting. Better than being like me who questions everything and doesn't trust most people," her sister said.

Amy Sue scoffed at that. Just once she wanted to be the one who solved the problem rather than made it. "He isn't going to get away with this, is he?" she asked as she climbed into the passenger side of her SUV and Josie slid behind the wheel. When she didn't reply, she glanced over and saw the answer on her sister's face. "He's going to lie and they're going to believe him rather than me because he's Jack Marshall, an upstanding member of society who has a lot of money and influence."

Josie didn't respond right away. "It will depend on his alibi and how airtight it is. He must have found a way to be in both places. I want to see this neighborhood," she said as she drove away from the police department.

Amy Sue felt chilled even on the sunny warm day at the thought of going back to the scene. Why hadn't she listened to her intuition last night? She'd been spooked in that unfinished neighborhood. It had felt all wrong. She had actually thought about not getting out of the car last night. "I should have just gone to a hotel, but you know me. I paid for a cute little apartment and was determined to stay there even though the area gave me the creeps."

"Things often happen for a reason," Josie said. "If you hadn't been scammed and gone to that address, you wouldn't have witnessed the murder, and Jack Marshall would have gotten away with it."

She couldn't help scoffing. "It looks like he'll get away with it anyway."

"Give the detectives a chance," Josie said. "In your statement, you said the neighborhood is under construction. I'm curious as to who is involved in the project."

"You think Jack Marshall might be one of the investors?"

"Probably not. But I'm betting some friend of his is. He had a key or at least knew the door would be open to the house you described. He planned this. He would have checked out the place beforehand. He'd know about the plastic sheeting. To pull this off, he'd been prepared— right down to disposing of the body and nailing down his alibi."

She couldn't help the shudder at the thought of how well-planned this murder had to have been as they drove south of Billings proper. No wonder the police hadn't believed her. She could hardly believe it herself.

Now in the daylight she could see that she'd been right. All of the structures in this cul-de-sac appeared to be under construction. A large sign read Johnstone Construction in front of one of the houses. Would the police look for a connection between Jack Marshall and this project?

There was no crime scene tape stretched across the entrance to the cul-de-sac. Nor was there any sign of police cars. Amy Sue felt her stomach churn. Of course not, since the cops didn't believe anyone had been murdered here by one of the leading businessmen in the city. By the time they'd arrived, Jack Marshall had already covered his tracks and was long gone.

"That's the house and apartment building next to it," she told her sister as Josie slowly drove around the loop to stop next to the larger of the two buildings. Around the cul-de-sac, other structures were in varying degrees of construction. She parked and turned off the engine before looking over at her.

"You don't have to go, but I'd like to look around," Josie said.

For a moment, Amy Sue hesitated, but reminded herself that she was a lot stronger than she thought she was. Isn't that what her grandmother used to tell her? After what she'd been through, maybe it was true.

She opened her door and climbed out, blinking in surprise at how different the area looked in the daylight. Beyond the new subdivision, there were open fields. In the distance was downtown Billings. Last night with the low clouds, she hadn't seen any lights. Nor was there anyone around this early in the morning. The construction crews wouldn't be arriving for a few hours yet—if they worked on a Sunday. Unless you knew what had happened here, a person wouldn't think there was anything scary about this place.

"Around back," she told her sister, and couldn't help glancing up at the second-story balcony where Jack Marshall had stood watching her drive off last night. She hugged herself against the chilly June morning as she hurried after her sister.

Chapter Three

Josie looked around as she walked between the narrow apartment building and the house built so close next to it. She hadn't seen any of this coming. That still surprised her. But since her fall and head injury, she no longer sensed trouble. It had been a relief to "see" nothing wrong.

But because of that she hadn't thought anything of her sister going to a weeklong class in Billings. She'd actually been happy that Amy Sue was getting back out there after what she'd been through the past year. Sensing nothing amiss, she hadn't been able to warn her.

"Start at the beginning and tell me exactly what you saw from the time you pulled up in front of the address you'd been given," the attorney in Josie said.

She watched her sister take a breath and let it out. "It was really dark last night," Amy Sue said, her voice cracking a little with obvious strain. Maybe it had been a mistake bringing her back here. Her sister was still shaken. "It looks so…different in the daylight."

As Josie walked, she hated that Amy Sue might be right about the car dealer never standing trial for the murder. The police hadn't believed there had even been a murder. Josie hated to think they might never know who the victim was let alone who had killed her. Given Jack Marshall's alibi, it made even Josie question if her sister had actually seen what she thought she had. Amy Sue had fallen in love for the first time last year and almost died at the hands of a killer. Because of that trauma, she worried that her sister couldn't trust her instincts.

But there was nothing wrong with her eyesight, Josie reminded herself.

"I thought I had the wrong address," Amy Sue said as if reliving it. "Even in the dark, I saw that the structures weren't finished. I felt spooked, but I'd paid good money for the place and…" She shook her head. "I know I should have just left and gone to a hotel, but I'd seen a photo of this cute little apartment… You must think I don't have any good sense at all."

"You wanted to believe that the apartment you rented for a week hadn't been a scam," Josie said as they reached the corner of the building. "Completely understandable." For as long as Josie could remember, she'd encouraged her sister to listen to her instincts. If Amy Sue had last night, she'd have gone to hotel and missed seeing a murder. Josie could imagine how scary this place might have felt last night without any street or porch lights or illumination coming from any of the buildings.

She turned to see her sister tense as they went around the back of the apartment house. The rear portion of the house and a large window on the second floor came into view. "Where were you standing?"

Amy Sue moved past the recessed door to the back of the apartment house and pointed out the door and the entry pad on the wall that she'd stumbled into. "I was digging in my purse. I'd tossed my phone in, and of course it had gone to the bottom of the bag. That's when I heard vehicles and then voices before I saw a light come on next door at the house."

Josie glanced at the window at the rear part of the house where her sister had seen the murder. Given the short distance, it was no wonder Amy Sue had been able to describe both of the people she saw—the late twenties to early thirties blonde woman and Jack Marshall, a man in his early forties. This spot had given her sister a front-row seat to witness a murder.

But what gave Josie pause was that the killer would have been able to see Amy Sue just as clearly after she'd accidentally switched on the back light.

It was exactly as her sister had described it to the police—the room in the house had open studs and was clearly still under construction. The only thing missing was the plastic that had hung over the one visible doorway.

"One more thing," Josie and, walked over to the back of the house, not surprised to find the door locked and the lockset requiring a key. Unless he'd had someone leave the door open, Jack Marshall had a key that he'd used to get inside.

Turning to her sister, she said, "I've seen enough. Let's go."

Amy Sue looked relieved as they walked to her car. "He's going to get away with murder, isn't he?"

Josie feared her sister was right as they got in the car. Jack Marshall hadn't left any evidence, including the body. "Come on, Sis, let's give the detectives a chance," she said as she started the engine "The killer made a mistake last night. He didn't expect anyone to be around."

She glanced over at Amy Sue, wanting to believe it. "He would have been rattled last night almost getting caught, which means he could have made yet another mistake. There is seldom a perfect murder, especially with the latest forensics."

"But don't you have to be actually investigating the murder for that to happen?" There was an edge to Amy Sue's voice that worried her. "I keep thinking about that moment when our eyes met. There was surprise, but not fear. I know now what I saw was arrogance. He killed that woman, and he knew he was going to get away with it. I hope you're right about him having made another mistake last night. I can't stand the thought that he might not be brought to justice."

It was Jack Marshall's arrogance that worried Josie. The man had seen Amy Sue. He'd seen her car, might even have gotten her plate number. With his connections he would be able to find her easily enough if he was worried the eyewitness was going to be trouble.

Josie suspected Jack Marshall had gotten rid of one problem and gotten away with it. What would keep him from getting rid of another one if Amy Sue became a problem?

Detective Russell Tate watched the SUV return with the two women. He'd been on his way to his patrol SUV but now stopped in the shadow of the police station, curious about them both. It was Amy Sue Brand, though, who had him wondering exactly what she saw last night. She didn't seem like the type to make something like that up out of thin air, especially given all the details she'd provided.

Yet Jack Marshall couldn't have killed anyone in Billings last night. He had an alibi, not that he needed it since there hadn't been any sign of a murder. Nor so far was there a report of a missing woman—let alone a stabbed to death one. Russ had checked because Amy Sue Brand had seemed like such a credible witness.

It wasn't like other people hadn't come in off the street with stories they'd concocted. Some just wanted attention. Others had a bone to pick. He wondered if Amy Sue Brand might have a reason to want to see Jack Marshall behind bars. Wouldn't hurt to do a little digging. Maybe there was a connection between the two even if it was no more than she'd bought a car from him.

He watched the two women drive away together in the younger sister's SUV before going back inside. At his desk, he realized that something about Amy Sue Brand had gotten to him. He pulled his keyboard closer. He needed to know about her, because something was definitely wrong about all of this.

What he found was exactly what the woman had told them. After growing up on a ranch out of Dry Gulch, Amy Sue now lived and worked on the family ranch. He found a few articles from high school. She'd been in the business club, belonged to both Future Farmers of America and Future Homemakers of America, and had never married nor had any children. She helped out with local fundraisers by bringing homemade baked or canned goods. From what he could see of the newspaper and Facebook photographs, she'd won blue ribbons with her baking and canning at the county fair.

Russ smiled to himself at he studied a young smiling Amy Sue looking shyly at the camera as she held up a blue ribbon for her pickled beets. There was such a clean, innocent look to her. She looked as if she couldn't tell a lie to save herself.

"What are you doing?" Detective Hanson said as he glanced at Russ's computer screen.

"I can't help being curious," he said.

"Those big blue doe eyes get to you? Or was it her figure?" His partner scoffed. "You do have a weakness for the crazy ones." Turning, he said over his shoulder, "I'm going home to get some sleep. You should do the same. We investigated, we found nothing in that house or on the premises. Jack Marshall wasn't there, and no one was murdered. Leave this and Marshall alone, or you'll be looking for a new job and me another partner," Hanson said, and left the room, slamming the door behind him.

Russ sat for a moment, smarting over that dig about the kind of women he fell for. "Thanks, Hanson, you're such a compassionate guy. Really appreciate it," he said to himself, and sighed as he thought of his ex. Maybe his partner was right about his last girlfriend, but Hanson was wrong about Amy Sue Brand. His gut told him that she'd seen what she said she had. What would it hurt to do a little more investigating?

While he was at it, he wanted to look into Jack Marshall as well. New to the department and the area, he was more than curious about the man from the television car ads. He'd never seen an eyewitness's accusation dropped so quickly by a police department. Hanson had been clear enough. Marshall was off-limits. He knew that even as he typed the man's name into his computer. Marshall was more than just a car salesman. He was a local legend.

What came up proved just how right he was. Jack

Marshall's smiling face appeared in article after article. An obvious do-gooder, he and his wife were involved in numerous benefits and even more organizations. Photo after photo of the pair dressed to the nines, smiling benevolently at the camera.

He definitely got it now. Jack Marshall was someone in this community, someone who could possibly commit murder and get away with it.

As he heard Hanson headed his way again, Russ quickly cleared his computer screen. He understood why his partner had told him to drop this. Hanson was from here and had been on the force for almost fifteen years. The cop knew what kind of trouble Russ could get in digging into Jack Marshall's life.

The unemployed kind.

AMY SUE HAD hoped that once she returned to the family ranch, she could try to forget what she'd witnessed. She loved it here, loved growing things, but she also knew she stayed because it had always been a safe place.

Until she invited the wrong man to the ranch.

Since then, she felt off-balance even here on the ranch she loved. As she began to wash the early batch of spinach for dinner, she couldn't believe that it was just a few weeks ago that she decided to attend the weeklong farmers co-op class in Billings and get out of her comfort zone.

She'd actually been excited. Even Josie had been encouraging for her to get out and do things on her own after she lost all confidence in herself last year. Who wouldn't start questioning themselves after falling in love with the wrong man and almost getting herself and her sister killed?

Since returning from Billings, though, she'd found she was second-guessing herself about everything and much worse than before. Maybe she hadn't seen what she thought she had that night in Billings. Was it possible the man had just looked like Jack Marshall? What if she was wrong and had accused an innocent man?

Putting the spinach into the strainer, she let out a curse. *She wasn't wrong.* She knew what she'd seen. She knew whom she'd seen. But the police didn't believe her—just as Jack Marshall had known they wouldn't. He'd made sure of that. She thought of him standing on the balcony at that house, that almost mocking look on his face. *Run to the cops and see where it gets you.*

She'd watched him in her side mirror as she was driving away to get to the police. She recalled how unhurried he'd been, as if he hadn't just killed a woman and there hadn't been an eyewitness because he knew the police would believe him—not her.

"Is everything okay?"

Amy Sue turned, surprised to see her sister, then shocked to realize how late in the day it was. "You're home already?" Lately, Josie had been staying more often in her room at the old farmhouse even though she had an apartment in town over her law office and lived at the newly renovated hotel with her husband. Amy Sue knew her sister staying at the ranch meant she was worried about her.

Josie reached past her to shut off the water she'd left running in the sink. "You looked as if you were miles away."

"Not so many miles actually," Amy Sue said as she put the spinach in a pot on the stove, then checked the beef roast in the oven. "Dinner's almost ready." She felt Josie come up behind her and put her arms around her.

"Would it help to talk to someone about it?" her sister asked. "Witnessing something like you did would be hard for anyone to get over."

"It wasn't witnessing the murder," Amy Sue snapped. "It's knowing he's escaping justice. I know what he did because I saw him do it. I saw his expression. He knew the police wouldn't believe me. He killed that woman. How do I live with that?"

"The law isn't always fair," Josie said. "Not everyone gets justice. But I do believe that you reap what you sow."

Amy Sue continued as if she hadn't heard what her sister said. "I should have stayed there and called the cops from my car," she said, chiding herself for being so terrified that she'd left and let him get away with murder—not to mention getting rid of the woman's body.

"No, you shouldn't have stayed," Josie snapped. "Do you really think he would have let you just sit there in your vehicle waiting for the cops to arrive? He was counting on your panic, on your fear of him, and why wouldn't you be afraid of a man who you'd just watched murder a woman?"

Amy Sue could feel the heat of her anger and frustration. She already knew what Josie would say before she said the words. "I can't let him get away with murder. If the police aren't going to do anything, then I have to."

"Okay," her sister said in a conciliatory tone. "You're angry and upset, but you need to let the police handle it.

Consider the man you want to bring to justice and how dangerous he is."

"Exactly. That's why I can't let it go. The cops either think I lied or was mistaken. Either way I can't walk away from this. Like you said, there was a reason I was there that night and witnessed that woman's murder, and it wasn't to do nothing about it."

Her sister fell silent for a few moments as she always did when she was about to say something Amy Sue wasn't going to like. "Forgive me for asking this, but how are you planning to go about bringing Jack Marshall to justice?"

It was a good question, one she hadn't worked out yet, but that didn't stop her. The moment she opened her mouth, she knew she'd been thinking about this ever since she'd returned home. "I'll find out everything there is to know about him, including who that woman was and why he killed her. I'll talk to everyone who gave him an alibi, people who work for him, people he fired. I'll dig up whatever dirt I can find until I ultimately prove he lied."

"And while you're doing that you do realize he'll hear about it," Josie said, clearly trying to reason with her.

"Good, I want him to know I'm not going to quit until the truth comes out," she said defiantly.

"He'll have you thrown in jail for stalking him. Worse, you could get yourself killed. He's already murdered one woman that we know of. What makes you think he wouldn't come after you?" Josie clutched her arm. "Please, really think about it before you do anything."

Christine Marshall could tell by her husband's mood what had happened.

It wasn't like she hadn't gone through this before. Not to mention, if the man was anything, he was more transparent than he thought. Then again, she also knew him so well. "Is everything all right?" she asked, knowing it wasn't.

"Fine."

She didn't bother to listen to the rest of his excuses for his behavior since his latest breakup two weeks ago. Christine always took some satisfaction in knowing that he would no longer be seeing whatever woman he'd been with the past few months. She could always tell when it was over. Usually, though he seemed freer, more relieved, more relaxed. Often after one of his affairs, he came back to her almost joyous.

What was different this time? she wondered. Maybe this time the woman had broken it off with him. That would be something new.

She found Jack's extracurricular activity of little interest. Her own life was full of what made her happy as the wife of such a prominent, powerful man. A lot of ambitious men had affairs. Her mother had warned her the first time Christine had brought Jack Marshall home.

He's going to be just like your father. He's far too handsome, far too ambitious, far too charismatic. He's going to need other women temporarily and if you want this marriage to last, you'll have to accept that graciously.

And Christine had, because rocking the boat would mean destroying their very public life, and she enjoyed the fruits of being married to Jack Marshall. She knew he'd married her for her money and her blue-blooded family name. Both had helped him rise quickly in stature, providing them with a very nice lifestyle that made even her closest well-to-do friends envious.

It was a fair trade-off, she told herself as she watched her husband leave for work and tried not to worry. But something was definitely different his time. For a moment, she feared that Jack might have fallen in love with this latest one.

She wasn't, however, fool enough to ever ask. Jack didn't seem to know that she knew about his extracurricular activities. Nor was she worried about Jack ever asking for a divorce. So even if he had fallen for someone else, she assured herself, he would never destroy the perfect life they'd built together. It was why Jack was so discreet. For fear of losing her and this life, the last thing he'd ever want was for her to find out what he did with the other women, she thought as he headed down the drive on his way to work.

As he neared the end of the drive, Jack looked back to where she was standing watching him leave. He seemed startled for a moment, clearly surprised that she had walked out to the veranda as if to wave goodbye. He smiled and called back to her, "Have a good day!"

She smiled and waved as he drove away, again telling herself that whatever was bothering her husband would pass. There was nothing to worry about.

Chapter Four

Jack Marshall glanced at his watch impatiently. He had better things to do than sit in an uncomfortable chair in an interrogation room at the police department. He'd thought the detective was joking when he'd gotten a call to come down to the station for a formal statement.

"If this is about what some woman thought she saw, I already told you, I was in Great Falls," he'd argued. "I can't believe you're taking any of what she said seriously. Was anyone actually killed?"

"We just need to get it on the record," Detective Hanson had said with a sigh. "The woman's attorney is pressuring us."

Once at the station, Hanson hurried him into an interrogation room and closed the door. There was another detective already waiting. Hanson introduced his new partner, Detective Russell Tate, and said, "Let's just get this over with."

Jack took a seat as Hanson put the date and time into the video recorder and named those present in the room, Jack Marshall and the two detectives.

"How is it that this eyewitness swears she saw you in Billings committing murder?" Detective Tate asked quickly, his partner shooting him a warning look.

"How should I know?" Jack snapped. "Clearly the woman is delusional or has something against me. Who is this woman anyway?"

"Amy Sue Brand of Dry Creek, Montana," Hanson said, and Tate groaned his disapproval with his partner revealing it. "The man has a right to know who's accusing him of murder," his partner said in Marshall's defense.

Jack decided he liked Hanson and would remember him if he ever needed a detective's help. He'd also remember the other one, the cowboy fresh off the range. The man clearly didn't know how things worked around here, but he better learn quickly, or Jack would see that he was back on the ranch. "I've never heard of her."

"Maybe you sold her a lemon of a car," Hanson suggested with a laugh.

Detective Tate jumped in, "Are you involved in the development under construction in the following area where the alleged murder took place?" He read the address.

"No," Jack snapped. "This is a total waste of my time."

"Do you know the developer? Thomas Armstrong?" Tate asked.

"I know a lot of people. Are we about done here?"

"We'll need your sworn statement that you were in Great Falls the night of the incident," Hanson said with a sigh.

"Also you might want to add that you didn't murder a woman that night," Detective Tate said, and got another dirty look from his partner. "For the record."

"Fine." Jack repeated his story, adding the part about not murdering anyone, followed by a curse. Getting to his feet, he gave them both an annoyed look. "Waste of taxpayers' dollars." He hoped they both got the veiled threat. He could get rid of both of them and maybe he would, he thought as he stormed out.

But he wasn't going to make waves until this blew over.

And it would blow over, not that it made him any less angry that it had happened. He'd run through the plan for several weeks before that night. True, the woman had forced his hand, requiring him to move up her demise more quickly than he would have liked.

Still, he'd been meticulous, always had when it came to the important decisions in his life. His father had taught him not to rush things. *Take your time. Do it right.*

He'd gone over the plan a dozen times before he set it in motion. It had been flawless, and it would have gone off without a hitch if it wasn't for that horrible woman showing up at the apartment next door when she had.

Once outside now, he climbed into the large luxury car with the dealer plates and tried to relax. It was over. The woman was mistaken about what she'd thought she'd seen and who she thought she'd seen, he told himself. The police hadn't believed anything she'd said; how could they? There was no body. No sign of a murder. And most important, he'd been out of town at the time. The only conclusion they could reach was the one he needed them to: Amy Sue Brand was delusional.

It was nice of Detective Hanson, but he hadn't even needed him to provide him with the name of the eyewitness. It hadn't taken much to find out who she was after he'd memorized her license plate number. He had a friend who often ran plate numbers for him on trade-ins. He liked to know who he was dealing with.

And now he did. Amy Sue Brand of Dry Gulch, Montana. A country girl with the most innocent face he'd ever seen. No wonder the cowboy cop had questioned him the way he had. Against all reason, Detective Tate had bought her story. Jack hoped the detective didn't become a problem—or Amy Sue Brand, either.

Back at the dealership, he sat down behind his desk and tried to breathe. He'd been feeling anxious since the phone call at the Great Falls hotel, first from his wife and then the Billings cops. Not that he hadn't been ready for it. He'd been expecting the call after that foolish woman had seen what he'd done. But he'd thought that would be the end of it.

After today, he tried to assure himself it would be over. He'd given the police the statement they wanted. He shouldn't be bothered again. So why didn't he believe it? Because his superstitious grandmother always swore that bad news came in threes. The eyewitness was number one. If number two was having to make a statement at the police department, then he couldn't wait for number three.

He told himself he was bulletproof. He was *somebody* and not just in this town. He was known across the northwest. Everyone knew Jack Marshall, recognized him from his television ads, had bought cars from him for years. He smiled and felt himself relax a little. As much as he enjoyed the money and what it bought him, he also liked being recognized on the street. People felt they knew him and came up to shake his hand.

He wished his father had lived long enough to see

the life he'd made for himself. Jack had a beautiful, sophisticated wife from a wealthy old family. But he also had all the women he wanted as long as he wanted them.

His smile faltered as he thought of the eyewitness who had recognized him. *"Looks like your celebrity status came back to take a bite out of your ass,"* he could hear his father say from his grave.

Jack mentally shook himself. He had to do something to get his mind off all of this. Not someone new, not this quickly, he told himself. But as he looked up from his glassed-in office, he spotted a pretty young brunette running a hand over the expensive car in the showroom as if she were petting a puppy.

He had a policy that he never mixed business with pleasure, but today he needed a distraction. He rose, adjusted his tie and stepped out of his office. "Like her?" he asked the brunette caressing the expensive car.

The woman's smile was dazzling. "I do."

"I normally leave this part up to my employees, but I feel like breaking the rules today. Want to take her out for a spin?" She hesitated, and he flashed her his famous smile. "Not everyone can handle a car like this, but I have a feeling you can."

She laughed. "You think?"

"Let me get the keys and a dealer plate," he said, then hesitated. "Sorry, I didn't get your name."

"Tina." He started to introduce himself, but she stopped him with a laugh. "Everyone knows who you are, Mr. Marshall."

"Call me Jack."

Chapter Five

"I got a call from the landowner at that new construction project," Detective Hanson said later that afternoon. He motioned for his partner to join him in an empty interrogation room. The moment the door closed behind them, his partner demanded, "What are you doing asking for the key to that house in the new subdivision to have another look around?"

"There's something about this case that bothers me," Russ said with a shrug.

"There is *no* case," Hanson snapped.

"The call you got from the landowner, did you happen to ask him how well he knows Jack Marshall?"

Hanson let out a string of curses. "Look, the chief wants this forgotten. It looks bad for the department as well as for an upstanding local businessman with far-reaching connections. I'm warning you. Leave this alone."

"Doesn't this whole thing make you a little suspicious?"

His partner let out an irritated grunt. "I could tell Ms. Brand got to you, but she's a nutjob. There was no murder. The man has an airtight alibi. Come on, Russ, there is no smoking gun."

"He killed her with a knife, and we never really checked his alibi out."

"Seriously? I just said there was no murder. I hope I don't have to keep telling you that. We aren't going to spend taxpayers' dollars chasing a murder that didn't happen."

Russ wished he could back away from it. But his doubts kept him awake at night. Yes, Amy Sue Brand had been more than a little rattled and upset, but who wouldn't be if she'd just witnessed a murder? It was odd that she'd ended up in that new addition when there obviously wasn't a place to rent. But she wouldn't be the first person to get scammed online.

Why would she make up a story like that? He didn't think she would. After digging into both Marshall and Brand, he hadn't found any connection between them. She'd never purchased a car from him, never even had one worked on at his dealership, and it appeared that the two had never met. Nor did they seem to share any relatives or friends. Their more than a decade's difference in age would have kept them from any high school rivalries even if Billings and Dry Gulch played sports at some point.

So, if it wasn't personal, what would her motivation be to accuse an innocent man of murder? It made no sense. Watching the woman during the interview, he didn't believe it was personal. Nor had her testimony wavered. She'd sworn the killer was Jack Marshall even when told he had an airtight alibi. What hurt her testimony was the lack of a body. There was no reason to believe a murder had even been committed by anyone, let alone Jack Marshall.

During his late-night arguments with himself, Russ admitted that he should forget about it and move on. If Amy Sue Brand was wrong about the man she swore was the killer, didn't that mean she was wrong about everything else since so far not only had a dead body not turned up but there hadn't been a report of a missing woman?

Except he kept seeing her the night she came into the police department to report the crime she'd witnessed not forty-five minutes before. Russ remembered the shock and terror on her bloodless face. He'd been haunted by the pain he'd seen in those blue eyes ever since.

AMY SUE HATED to admit that her sister was right. How could she even go about proving what she'd seen? Jack Marshall had money, influence and an airtight alibi, and he had destroyed or hidden any evidence including the woman's body.

Because there was no sign of a crime, Amy Sue appeared irrational, confused, untrustworthy. Add to that Marshall's alibi—he wasn't even in town the night of the murder hence she couldn't have seen him.

He couldn't have made her look more foolish for accusing him. But that wasn't what ate at her. There would be no justice for the woman he'd killed. The odds were too against it. Amy Sue couldn't put it out of her mind. She kept seeing the murder as if in slow motion and stewing over the police not taking her seriously and arresting Jack Marshall.

With a curse, she told herself she just needed to go into Dry Gulch for some supplies to get her mind off it. Her sister was right. What could she do, if the police weren't going to act? Nothing.

Once in her SUV and driving down the road toward town, she did feel a little better. On each side of the road was land that had been in the family for years. She took in the familiar landscape. It made her feel safe and protected.

Her sister thought she was trapped here, obviously not realizing how much she loved this ranch. Their grandmother had always believed that Amy Sue would be the one who would choose to leave. That was why Gram had left the ranch to Josie, so the place would always stay in the family.

It was hurtful. But she'd never shared the bond Josie did with their gram. She'd always believed it was because her sister had their grandmother's second sight and she didn't. But maybe it was because her grandmother didn't trust her youngest granddaughter to be capable of the responsibility. After all, hadn't Josie always gotten her out of trouble even when they were growing up and even more recent than that?

Maybe they were right not to trust Amy Sue, since she'd made some bad decisions lately. Like the night of the murder. Why hadn't she listened to that spooked part of her? Why hadn't she turned around and gone to a hotel the moment she sensed something was wrong?

When she'd left that subdivision, she'd been running scared. She should have driven just far enough away to call the police and make sure he didn't get away. Maybe the cops would have gotten there in time to catch Jack Marshall loading the woman's body into his fancy SUV.

She realized she was obsessing all over again. The

idea of driving into town was to get her mind off the murder. She hadn't even been paying attention, because she was startled and had to swerve when a large SUV came roaring up behind her going too fast. From the tracks in the muddy road behind her, she could see that the SUV had just come off the ranch road. What had the driver been doing on her property? And now the driver was riding her bumper trying to get around her.

As soon as she pulled over a little to let him pass, instead of shooting past her, the driver slowed to come alongside her. She looked over, a curse on her lips until she got a look at the man behind the wheel.

Shock sent her pulse racing at even the sight of Jack Marshall again. But when he pointed his index finger at her like a gun and pretended to pull the trigger she was so startled, so astonished, that she swerved. The left-hand front tire caught in the soft earth at the edge of the rural road and pulled her toward the ditch. It took all of her strength to get her vehicle back on the road.

By then Jack Marshall had sped off, disappearing over the horizon.

Shaking badly, she hit her brakes, coming to an abrupt stop in the middle of the road as she tried to calm down. She gripped the wheel, fighting to rein in her emotions. It was scary enough that the man had been on their ranch. But he'd actually threatened her? She couldn't believe this was happening.

She'd thought that if she could put it out of her mind, she could accept there was nothing more she could do. But he'd come to her ranch. He'd threatened her. At first, she had wanted to turn around and race back to the ranch house where she'd always felt safe. She knew she'd been hiding there for years, but especially after last year.

As the initial shock waned, she felt her anger boil up. This man thought he could intimidate her. Why? So she would take back her statement to the police? Or to keep her from causing him any more trouble? Either way, it made her furious.

She'd already had one man lie, manipulate and ultimately threaten her. Not this time, she swore to herself. Jack Marshall thought no one could take him down. While he might be right about that, Amy Sue was damned sure going to try.

DETECTIVE RUSSELL TATE had always loved a good mystery. It was why he'd gone to the academy and worked his way up to detective. His family hadn't understood why he would leave his life on the ranch outside of Roundup, let alone become a cop.

"You sure one of those wild horses you're always trying to break didn't kick you in the head?" his brother Patrick joked.

"Leave him be," their father said. "The ranch will always be here when he's ready to come back." John Russell Tate Sr., just assumed the day would come when his youngest son would get so lonesome for wide-open spaces, the smell of horseflesh and leather beneath him that he'd come back home. "He's got to try somethin' different to be sure of where he belongs."

"You can take the cowboy to the city, but you can't take the cowboy out of a man," his mother Maggie had said with a laugh.

Russ always took the good-natured kidding with a

smile because it was true. It came with the territory. A lot of his friends had left the state for an education or a better job. A lot of ranchers had to sell because their offspring had no desire to ranch.

Russ was a cowboy through and through. He had no idea what the future held, just that right now he was also a cop and he had a mystery, one he was determined to solve.

The way he saw it Amy Sue Brand had seen a murder, but the killer wasn't Jack Marshall. Or the woman was confused as his partner was determined to believe. Or Jack Marshall killed the blonde just as the Brand woman had said and now Marshall was going to get away with it, if Russ didn't figure out how he did it.

He realized he was leaning toward believing the eyewitness. Jack Marshall had a pretty tight alibi, though. He would have had to set it all up long before the murder. He'd apparently gotten the woman to the construction site and killed her, using the plastic available to leave no evidence of the crime. But wasn't he in Great Falls at the time? And how had he gotten rid of the body so quickly?

Russ felt a shock as a thought struck him like a horseshoe upside the head. The killer had left no evidence of the crime behind, except for the missing sheets of plastic from the room where Amy Sue said she'd seen him kill the woman. Russ had no doubt that the plastic had been on the floor and doorways the night Amy Sue had seen the murder—no matter what the contractor said. But again, he had no proof.

But what had come to him was how perfect it was to kill the woman at a construction site at night where there'd been a lot of excavation. It was the perfect place to bury a body quickly.

All Russ needed was a cadaver dog to search the area.

He stood up and walked to the chief's office and tapped on his door. A gruff "Come in" was emitted from the other side. Opening the door, Russ stepped in.

The chief, Milton "Milt" Westmoreland had the face of an overweight bulldog and was known for his bite as well as his bark. "What now, Tate?"

"I'm going to need a cadaver dog," he said, adding, "Sir," a little late. "I want to search that construction site where the woman saw the murder. It's the perfect place to get rid of a body quickly."

"There was no murder," the chief said through gritted teeth.

"Maybe," Russ said. "Or maybe not, sir. But don't you think it's worth at least seeing what we find? If I don't find a body or any evidence at the site, then I won't mention it again."

"You won't mention it again because I'm telling you not to. I won't have you out there looking for a body, wasting taxpayers' money and my time, let alone calling even more attention to this. I'm warning you, Tate. Drop it. You are treading on thin ice as it is. I don't want to hear another word about this. I especially don't want to hear the name Jack Marshall for any reason. Am I making myself clear enough for you?"

Russ stood for a moment, wanting to argue but seeing it wasn't going to get him anywhere. He'd have to come at this from another direction. "Yes, sir." With that, he turned and left, closing the door behind him but not before hearing the chief swearing up a storm in his wake.

He was going to have to wait until the body turned up. Or someone reported a woman missing. Neither had happened yet. Maybe he'd find a connection between the dead woman and Jack Marshall—if only he had a name.

If Amy Sue was right about all of it, then the man had known exactly what he was doing and had covered his tracks well. What nagged at Russ was that if Marshall had pulled off the perfect murder, Amy Sue wouldn't have accidentally been at the scene that night and witnessed it. No one would have known there was even a murder, and Jack Marshall would have never been accused—if not for Amy Sue accidentally being there.

It always came back to the same thing. If Amy Sue told the truth and saw what she believed she had, then Jack Marshall had made a mistake by killing the woman in what should have been the perfect place. And if so, maybe he had made another mistake, one he hadn't realized yet? One Russ hadn't discovered yet.

He couldn't give up, even knowing what it could cost him if he continued to pursue this.

AMY SUE FOUND the tracks where Jack Marshall had driven into the back road to the ranch house. Because of the rain the night before, it was easy to follow the tire tracks. She hadn't gone far before she saw where he had turned onto the side road that led to the back of the house.

Her heart began to pound harder as she followed his trail, knowing where he'd gone even before she'd seen the spot where he'd pulled over and gotten out.

From where he'd parked, she could see the roofline of the farmhouse and wasn't surprised that his footprints had headed in that direction. Her blood thundered in her ears as she opened her door and stepped out. Avoiding his footprints, she walked alongside them to the outcropping of rocks on the hillside where he would have hidden, but had a clear view into her house.

She shuddered at the thought of him watching her through the curtainless windows. They lived in the country, miles from another house. They had no reason to close the curtains even at night. Knowing he had spied on her felt more dangerous than him pretending to shoot her. She felt violated just thinking of him watching her where she'd been standing in the kitchen earlier.

This wouldn't be the first time a killer had come to the ranch looking for her, she thought as she pulled out her phone and took photographs of his tracks in the earth.

But this time she knew the man was a killer—just as she knew that if she didn't stop him, it might be only a matter of time before he came back for her.

Chapter Six

Josie had never wanted her sister to be wrong about something so badly. "You're sure it was Jack Marshall you saw on the road?" she asked after Amy Sue rushed into her office and told her what had happened.

"*Really?*" Amy Sue said clearly exasperated. "You sound just like the police. You think I'm mistaken again? He pretended to shoot me. Believe or not, not all that many people want me dead."

"I'm sorry," Josie said quickly. "I just don't want to believe he would do something so…dangerous as to stalk his accuser."

"I told you he was arrogant. He knows I can't prove he murdered that woman, so he feels safe," Amy Sue said as she paced, too upset no doubt to sit.

Josie couldn't blame her. This was very upsetting news. Jack Marshall seemed, if not smart, at least extremely careful. Why would he chance being seen on their ranch by the eyewitness in an alleged murder? It made no sense unless…

"For him to take a chance like this, he's worried you'll make more trouble for him and that makes him dangerous," Josie said. "It's not against the law for him to come to the ranch, but it is definitely suspicious. Did you happen to get the license plate number on the car he was driving?"

"Dealer plates." Amy Sue told her, adding the make and model of the large black SUV. "The same cars he sells at his dealership."

"As your lawyer, I'll let the police know. They might want a statement from you and to see the photos you took of his tracks."

Her sister rolled her eyes. "What is the point?" she demanded. "You know he'll deny it or have a good reason to be near Dry Gulch, let alone on our ranch."

"They need to know in case we have to get a restraining order on him."

Amy Sue shook her head. "You've always said restraining orders aren't worth the paper they're printed on."

"I'm just trying to cover all the bases. It's what I do." Josie watched her sister finally drop into a chair across from her desk. Her voice also dropped as she said, "He's going to come after me, isn't he? That's what he was doing. Scoping out the place to make sure he has an airtight alibi the night he comes to kill me."

Josie rose from her desk to sit in the chair next to her. "He isn't going to kill you," she said, adding silently, *not yet anyway, I hope.* "Wouldn't it look suspicious if the eyewitness to the alleged murder he didn't commit suddenly ended up dead?"

"You seem to forget who we're dealing with."

"No, I haven't forgotten," she said. Amy Sue didn't know about the pressure she'd been putting on the police to investigate her sister's claim more fully. Now she wondered if it had backfired. Feeling pressure, Jack Marshall had come to the ranch to try to scare her sister off.

Was he the one running scared? Or was it more like her sister said? Was he planning his next murder? Josie didn't want Amy Sue to become a problem for the man given how he'd dealt with the last woman.

"I'm going to get security for the ranch," Josie said, surprised at Amy Sue's immediate response.

"Don't waste your money." Her sister shook her head and rose. "I'm not going to be there. I'm going to Billings, and I'm going to find proof that he killed that woman. I won't be safe until he's behind bars." She no longer looked scared or upset. She looked determined, which frightened Josie even more. She should be scared. Josie was.

"Don't try to talk me out of it. I'm obviously not safe here, and I'm not going to sit around and wait for him to come for me."

Josie understood her sister's frustration only too well. She also couldn't argue that she wasn't wrong about not being safe. Just as she knew what the police response would be to Jack Marshall coming to the ranch and spying on Amy Sue. The most the cops might do was talk to Marshall, which could make it even worse for her sister. Jack Marshall would deny it and get away with it—just as he had the murder.

But she wanted it on the record in case this got worse. "I don't want you to be another of the man's victims. We need to at least give the police a chance," Josie said reasonably. "Also if you could just wait until I'm finished with this trial up in Missoula, I'll help you." She had hoped that after a few days, a few weeks, her sister would change her mind. But after today, she could see that wasn't going to happen.

"The only reason I'm telling you is so you know where I've gone and get me out of jail if I need a lawyer."

"I'm more worried about you ending up dead than needing an attorney," Josie said truthfully. "Let's not forget that this man is a murderer. He's gotten away with at least one murder that we know of. What makes me think that he might not have done this before? Look how well he'd planned this murder. If you hadn't accidentally been there that night, no one would have seen anything and no one would have been the wiser."

Amy Sue stared at her. "If you really think he's done this before, then you know he'll do it again. Even if he doesn't come after me, he might have already found his next victim. I have to stop him. Someone has to nail the bastard." Josie saw tears welling in her sister's eyes. "The woman he killed? While I couldn't hear what was being said, I could tell what was going on. She looked so young and hopeful, as though he was showing her a house where they were going to live together. She was excited. I know what it's like wanting to believe in a man only to find out he's lying, or worse, wants you dead. If I can get this woman justice…"

She didn't have to finish. Josie knew that her sister wanted closure on her own near-death experience at the hands of a killer. She wasn't going to quit until she got it for the woman she saw killed. But it was her obvious determination that settled it. Once Amy Sue made up her mind about something, there was no changing it. "Do you have a plan?"

"I will," she said firmly. "Don't worry. I figure he'll

want to shut me up, but he can't kill me because that would look suspicious. Instead, he'll use his clout and the legal system to protect himself. Hopefully by the time he does, I'll have enough damning evidence to put him away before he resorts to murder again."

"I certainly hope you're right."

"You just worry about your big trial. I appreciate all the help you've already given me, but we both can't get arrested. Who'd get us out of jail?"

Josie couldn't help being proud of the woman her sister had become, but at the same time she was terrified how this might end. She wanted to try to talk her out of what she was thinking of doing but saved her breath at the look on Amy Sue's face. "Call if you need me." Otherwise, she feared, it could be the police calling her with bad news.

DETECTIVE TATE HADN'T been surprised to hear that attorney Josie Brand Lander was calling. She'd been badgering the chief as well as Detective Hanson and himself to take her sister's eyewitness murder report seriously.

He assumed this call was her wanting an update. He wished he had something to tell her as he answered his phone. Along with finding Amy Sue a reliable witness, he found her lawyer sister very sharp and competent. Like her sister, it didn't appear she was going to give up wanting to know the truth. Short of Jack Marshall in handcuffs, he doubted anything about her sister's claim was going to give her what she wanted.

"Jack Marshall wasn't just on our ranch, he threatened my sister." She went on to tell him the rest, her words coming as a shock.

Jack Marshall had gone out to Amy Sue Brand's ranch, actually parked, and spied on her and the house? Why would an innocent man do that? Nor did it sound like the man he'd come to know through the media. Jack wasn't just a celebrity, he was a prominent business-man with both social and political ties in high places. He shouldn't have even known about Amy Sue—unless he saw her the night of the murder and took down her license plate number.

With a silent curse, he recalled his partner telling Marshall the woman's name. Russ had later argued with Hanson about that.

"Doesn't he have the right to know who his accuser is?" Hanson had demanded. "How else could we find out if he knew of a grievance this woman might have against him?"

Still, Russ thought it more than risky and out of character for Marshall to go out to the Brand ranch, let alone apparently spy on Amy Sue and later threaten her. He wondered if the man would deny it when questioned. If not, what excuse would he come up with?

"I'm glad you called me about this," Russ told Josie.

"I'm aware it will again be a case of my sister's testimony against Jack Marshall's," she said. "But it concerns me. This man who claims he's innocent is suddenly so interested in my sister that he comes out to the ranch, parks where his rig can't be seen and watches her in our house? Later he makes a point of trying to scare her by pretending to shoot her?"

He listened as she explained that Amy Sue had taken photographs of his tracks in the damp earth from the spot where he had been watching the house with her visible inside. She asked for his cell phone number so she could send them to him. He gave it to her, afraid this was going to prove nothing.

Josie also gave him a description of the vehicle Marshall had been driving with the dealer plates. "This should concern you, detective, and make you as upset as it does me that he came anywhere near my sister. This is not the behavior of an innocent man. But it is the behavior of a man who believes he is above the law and thinks he can scare my sister into keeping her mouth shut. Doesn't that sound dangerous to you, Detective?"

"It does," Russ said. "I will definitely take it up with Mr. Marshall."

They fell silent for a few moments. "There is still nothing on the missing murdered woman?" she asked.

"I check missing persons every day. So far nothing. But I assure you, I am taking your sister's allegations seriously." He could hear in her tone that she questioned that. "Please don't hesitate to call me if anything else comes up."

"Until Jack Marshall is behind bars, you'll be hearing from me," she said, and hung up.

Russ replaced the receiver at his desk and looked at what the attorney had sent him on his cell phone. Tracks in the soft damp earth still couldn't prove that Jack Marshall had been there any more than Amy Sue swearing he'd threatened her. He didn't doubt that it had happened, but he needed solid evidence.

Again he checked for a missing woman about the age and description Amy Sue had supplied. Still nothing. He knew from experience that the body might not turn up for years—if at all. Montana had thousands of acres of mountains, rivers and ravines. Jack Marshall, who'd grown up in Billings, could know a lot of places to bury a body.

If the man was a killer and had taken the time to dispose of the body outside of Billings before returning to Great Falls. That was a lot of ifs.

More and more, Russ suspected Marshall had done it. The problem was proving it with his hands tied by the department. The only way he could dig deeper into Jack Marshall and his whereabouts on the night of the murder would require probable cause that a crime had been committed. Without a body or evidence, there was no way a judge would issue a warrant.

Chapter Seven

Amy Sue had wanted to come up with a plan before she reached Billings. Her ultimate mission to get justice seemed insurmountable as she drove into Montana's largest city. The noise, all the people and the traffic were bad enough, but she kept feeling the scope of Jack Marshall's reach here.

There'd been billboards on the way into the city. When she stopped for gas, she saw Jack Marshall's smiling face looking out at her from an ad in the newspaper. Once at the hotel, she spotted a flyer about some fundraiser he and his wife were attending next month. She was afraid to turn on the television for fear of seeing one of his car commercials.

The man was everywhere smiling into the camera, those mocking blue eyes daring her to come after him.

After unpacking, she felt at loose ends and questioned what she was doing here. She reminded herself that he'd come out to the ranch, trespassed and spied on her where she lived before threatening her. Anger replaced feeling as if she was in over her head. She knew she was, but she couldn't let that stop her. She found his address and left the hotel.

The Marshalls lived in a house on the edge of the

rock rims that circled the city. It was a pricey neighborhood, but Amy Sue would have expected nothing less. *Ostentatious* was the only word that described the massive house with its huge windows that looked out over the city. She parked on the street to study the house as if it could tell her what to do next.

Like her sister, she suspected the woman Jack Marshall killed had been a lover based on what she'd seen just before the murder. Did that mean that Jack's wasn't a happy marriage and that his perfect public life was a facade?

Why would the man take such a risk otherwise? she wondered. Look what he'd be giving up if he went to prison, not to mention toppling from the pedestal he now stood on. If she could prove what he'd done, he'd lose much more than just his freedom. His whole life would come crashing down—and so would his wife's.

She realized that he either got off on the danger, or he was so arrogant he thought he'd never get caught or maybe he couldn't help himself. No matter why he cheated let alone killed, Jack Marshall had an Achilles' heel. His weakness made her feel a little better.

One of the four garage doors opened at the house, and she watched as an expensive sleek car backed out. As the door closed, the driver headed in her direction, making her hurriedly pretend to dig in her purse for something as the car drove slowly past.

She managed to get a look at the wife. Mrs. Jack Marshall was so frequently photographed, usually alongside her husband, she was easily recognizable. Like her house, Christine was exactly what Amy Sue had expected.

The woman had an air of wealth and privilege as she

drove past. Her hair was cut in a perfectly sculpted short blond bob. Diamonds glittered at her earlobes. Huge sunglasses hid her eyes. She didn't give Amy Sue a glance as she turned onto the street and headed south.

Curious as to where the woman was going, Amy Sue shifted into gear and followed her. Even as she did, she questioned why. How could it possibly help prove ths woman's husband was a murderer? Still she kept driving, telling herself she had to know the lay of the land, which meant understanding the world Jack Marshall lived in.

She suspected the woman was meeting friends, attending some charity function meeting, getting a massage or her having her nails done. Dressed the way she was, the one thing she wasn't going to do was help her husband bury a body.

No surprise, Christine drove to what looked like a pricey salon. When she turned into a parking lot, Amy Sue did the same. As she watched Mrs. Marshall disappear inside, her cell phone rang.

"Hi, Josie," she said answering on the third ring.

"You promised to check in," her sister chided.

"I am. Right now, I'm about to go inside a very fancy hair salon to see about getting myself a new hairdo."

"That doesn't sound like you."

"Which is exactly what I should do. I'm tired of being me."

Silence, then, "You scare me when you talk like that," her lawyer sister said.

"Don't worry, I'm fine," she said. "Anyway, I'm in good company. Jack Marshall's wife Christine just went into the salon." Before her sister could try to talk her out of whatever she planned to do, she said, "Gotta go."

Disconnecting, she got out, headed for the salon door. She told herself that Jack wouldn't have told his wife about the eyewitness who accused him of murder, let alone admit that he'd gone out to her ranch to spy on her. Which meant Christine Marshall wouldn't recognize her.

As she pushed open the door and got her first scent of expensive hair products, she had a sudden thought. What if Jack's wife *did* recognize her?

Jack wouldn't have told her about Amy Sue accusing him of murdering the woman he'd been seeing. But if he had, that would put a different spin on things. But it seemed unlikely even if the wife knew about her husband's dalliances.

Amy Sue studied the elegantly dressed woman being led to a spot across from her in the salon. Christine chatted with the hairstylist like a woman who spent a great deal of time here, a woman who took good care of herself and had every reason to protect the fairytale life she and Jack had built.

CHRISTINE FELT THE woman's eyes on her. She was used to people noticing her. They often did a double take. Spending so much time as she did with charities and fundraisers and social events and the publicity that went with it, people recognized her. They would pass her on the street and stop walking, thinking they knew her. Not that she got as much attention as her husband, but then again, her face wasn't plastered all over the television screen as often as his.

Normally it didn't bother her when she felt someone staring at her. But after this morning, Jack and his latest affair had been on her mind more than usual. She couldn't shake the feeling that he'd become involved in a dangerous entanglement that would cause them both harm.

Feeling someone watching her, she had looked up and locked eyes with a young blonde woman. A prickle of alarm shot through her at the intensity of the woman's stare. Before the blonde dragged her gaze away, Christine glimpsed distress in the woman's eyes and quickly lowered her gaze.

The exchange had left her a little shaken. Was this one of Jack's old indulgences? Or the new one that had him acting so strangely? The blonde was young and certainly pretty enough, but looked almost too sweet for Jack. She didn't look like his type, unless he'd changed his preferences.

With a sliver of concern boring under her skin, she worried that this woman was the mistake he couldn't seem to shake.

That thought unsettled her for the rest of her appointment. She hadn't realized how upset she was until she chipped one of her nails on the salon chair and had to have it repaired before she could leave.

By then the blonde was gone, but not forgotten.

Worse, Christine feared she would see the young woman again.

AFTER SPENDING OVER a hundred dollars to have her hair shampooed and conditioned, trimmed and blown out, Amy Sue slid behind the wheel of her SUV, pulled her hair back up into a ponytail and left the salon having learned little, but with less money. Her hairstylist had told her how lucky she was that her booked appointment had cancelled. Amy Sue realized how true that was as she had glanced around the salon to see that all the clientele resembled Christine Marshall in varying degrees.

The only good that had come out of it was that she'd been able to watch Jack's wife from a couple of chairs away. Everything about the woman spoke of money and breeding. She was classically beautiful, clearly in great shape, living a pampered lifestyle. She didn't look like a woman who was aware that she had a cheating husband, let alone a murdering one.

She took the time to learn what she could about Christine Marshall online. From what she could gather, the woman had married beneath her. Jack didn't have the pedigree that his wife did. Nor did he have old wealth. But he had the looks and the drive. He'd been a star quarterback in high school and had gotten a scholarship to Montana State University in Bozeman. He'd made a name for himself in the state and after working at a small car dealership in Wyoming, he'd come back and taken over a struggling dealership.

He started the television advertising, using his good looks and charm to become a name and face people recognized. About that time, he met Christine. It wasn't clear if she put money into the dealership to build it up to what it was today. But the two of them became the most photographed couple in the city as they rose to the top of society.

From the outside, it was the American dream. Amy Sue could almost buy into this picture-perfect couple and probably would have if she hadn't seen Jack Marshall kill a woman.

Pocketing her phone, she thought of that moment when

Christine had looked up, their gazes locking. What she saw was curiosity, then concern, before Amy Sue looked away. Now both Marshalls could recognize her. She wasn't sure she'd helped her cause today.

Not that it was going to stop her. She thought of Jack Marshall coming to her ranch, spying on her, threatening her. As she started her SUV and pulled away from the salon, she drove toward the car dealership.

It was time to take this to the lion's den.

Jack had come to her ranch to scare her off. The least she could do was let him know she didn't scare that easily. Even as she thought it, though, her heart began to pound.

Detective Russell Tate stepped out of the abnormally hot June day into the car showroom, removing his Stetson as he did. He was greeted by a much-appreciated air-conditioned blast of chilled air. He stopped for a moment to breathe it in. The showroom sparkled from the glare of new car chrome. Past a hulking new black SUV, he spotted Jack Marshall's glass-enclosed office and headed for it.

Marshall looked up and frowned, not even bothering to hide how annoyed he was to see him.

Russ stuck his head in the open doorway. "Just need to ask you a couple of questions."

The car dealer shook his head with a curse. "What now?" he demanded, sounding more than a little irritated.

Stepping into the office, Russ took a chair in front of the man's desk even though he hadn't been offered one. He balanced his Stetson on his knee for a moment before pulling out his phone. "This is on the record, so I'll be recording it," he said as he hit Record. Before Marshall could object, he said, "Have you ever been out to the Brand ranch?"

"Of course not."

"Then you didn't go out there yesterday?"

"Didn't I just say that?" Marshall snapped.

"Amy Sue Brand not only saw you coming out of ranch property, but she followed your tracks and found a spot where you had gotten out of your vehicle to walk to where you had a view of her house and her through the windows."

"You can't be serious. What is it with this woman? Why would I do that?"

"That's what I want to know, since when she passed you on the road as your vehicle came out of a ranch road, she said you made sure she saw you. She said you pointed your finger like it was a gun and pretended to shoot her."

Marshall was on his feet. "I've had enough of this. You keep harassing me based on what this unhinged woman continues to make up about me and I will sue your department and see that you're walking a beat—if you're lucky."

"You aren't threatening an officer of the law, are you, Mr. Marshall?"

With a huge sigh, the man pointed at the door. "I won't be talking to you again without my lawyer present."

"If you feel it's necessary, Mr. Marshall, that is your right." Russ rose slowly but didn't shut off his phone's recorder. "Ms. Brand's attorney is considering a restraining order against you, so I'd suggest you not return to her ranch."

"I'm considering the same thing to stop you from harassing me, Detective. Don't show your face around here again."

Once in his patrol car, Russ called Josie. "Mr. Marshall denied all of it."

"Tell me you aren't surprised."

"Are you still considering taking out a restraining order?" Russ asked.

"Would it do any good?"

"Probably not," the detective had to admit. "He might see it as a dare." The lawyer said something under her breath. "I mentioned a restraining order hoping to keep him away from your sister. I'm sorry he threatened her."

"Not half as sorry as I am," she said. "Amy Sue isn't going to let this go. She's talked about doing some investigating on her own."

Russ rubbed the back of his neck. "That would be a mistake, but I'm sure you know that. If she's right about what she saw, Jack Marshall is a very dangerous man."

After a beat, she said, "*If* she's right?"

"I believe it's definitely worth investigating further."

She let out what sounded like a nervous laugh. "You sound like Amy Sue. I wouldn't be surprised if your paths cross soon. She's gone to Billings determined to get justice."

"I'm sure you told her what a bad idea that is?"

"Once my sister makes up her mind about something, it's next to impossible to dissuade her otherwise," the attorney said. "Good luck trying when you see her."

Chapter Eight

Sitting in his patrol SUV, Russ had just disconnected from his call with the lawyer when he saw her sister drive up. He was still upset with how his visit with Jack Marshall had gone and his conversation with attorney Josie Brand Lander.

He shouldn't have been surprised as he watched Amy Sue park and get out of her SUV to head toward the front door of the dealership. He hadn't expected their paths to cross so soon.

"This can't be good," he said to himself and, grabbing his Stetson, climbed out from behind the wheel to try to run interference.

Just inside the door, he spotted her looking at a black Cadillac convertible sitting in the showroom. "I took you for an SUV or pickup driver," he said, coming up beside her.

She turned, startled to see him. "Detective Tate." The woman got a lot into those two words. She thought that he didn't believe her, that he wasn't trying to find out the truth, that Jack Marshall was untouchable even from the law in this city.

She was right on only one of those. He was sticking his neck out and trying not to get fired because it would make it harder for him to prove Jack Marshall was a murderer and get the justice the dead woman deserved—if she was right about the man.

"Looking for a new car?" he asked.

"Sure, why not?"

He chuckled as he saw her gaze drift in the direction of Marshall's office. He noticed that the man had closed his blinds after their earlier visit, an indication he didn't want any more visitors today. Russ figured Amy Sue was the last person he would want to see and hated to think how ugly things could get. He didn't want to have to arrest her after Marshall called the chief.

"Can I interest you in lunch?" he asked and saw her surprise. He lowered his voice, moving a little closer. "I suspect we might be here for the same reason. Also you look hungry."

She frowned, took another glance at the closed blinds of Marshall's office and said, "I could probably eat something."

Once outside, he said, "Let's take your rig."

"Don't want to be seen with me?" she joked.

"Not for the reasons you're thinking," he admitted. He could well imagine what his boss would have to say about it. Wouldn't look good, the detective and the eyewitness fraternizing, even if there was no official case.

It wasn't until they were seated at a nearby fast-food restaurant in a back corner spot away from the other patrons who might come in that she asked, "Were you protecting me or Jack Marshall back there?"

"You. I'd already talked to him about being on your ranch. I left him in a bad mood. I figured you were safer having lunch with me."

"He denied it, didn't he?" She sighed and picked up her menu, not waiting for an answer.

"Your sister sent me the photos, but I'd like to see the ones you took."

She peeked out from behind the menu, eyeing him for a moment before she put it down and pulled out her phone. It took her only a few moments to call up the shots she'd taken. Without a word, she handed him the cell.

The first picture was of vehicle tracks. They could have been of any one of a dozen from Marshall's lot, so not helpful.

But the boot prints were definitely interesting. Those could be matched to a pair of Marshall's boots. Unfortunately, all it would prove though was that he'd lied about going out to her ranch, which Russ already knew. Amy Sue had seen him when he'd pretended to shoot her.

He handed back the phone as the waitress came by to take their orders. He doubted Amy Sue was no longer hungrier than he was, but they both ordered burgers loaded and iced tea, hers with lemon.

"What were you going to do at the dealership?" he asked after the waitress left to turn in their orders.

Another sigh, before she said, "Rattle his cage, why? Were you going to arrest me?"

He shook his head. "Your sister told me you were in town."

As if sensing Josie had told him a lot more than that, she said, "You think I'm way out of my depth trying to bring him to justice, don't you?" When he didn't answer at once, she added, "I am, but someone has to do it."

"What makes you think I'm not trying to do the same thing?"

She rolled her eyes. He noticed they were the color of the Montana summer sky. He had seen how attractive she was the night she'd come to the police station to report a murder. But sitting here facing him in the restaurant, he realized what it was about her that that he liked so much. She hadn't worn makeup, didn't need it. Maybe that added to the healthy glow he saw in that ingenuous face.

There was something so pure about her. The words *farm fresh* came to mind, and he almost laughed. She was too sweet and naive to go after a man like Jack Marshall, and that scared him.

She was staring at him, probably because she'd caught him staring at her.

"So, if you're investigating, does that mean you believe me?"

He couldn't miss the hope in her tone. As much as he would have loved to encourage that hope, he couldn't do it. "Let's just say, I have more questions than answers. I suspect you do, too."

"So you don't believe me. No wonder I didn't think the police were doing anything," she said, glancing away.

"*I* am looking into it. But I'm concerned that you are, too. I'd hate to see you put yourself in danger."

She chuckled, her gaze returning to hold his. "Why, Detective, would I be in danger? There was no murder, Jack Marshall was in Great Falls, and he's never killed a fly let alone a woman, so what would I have to fear?" Her blue eyes bored into him. "So why are *you* bothering to investigate if it never happened?"

"I'm a police detective. It's what I do."

She rolled her eyes again. "If you really are investigating, tell me something you've found out."

Russ told himself that he wouldn't be sharing police information he shouldn't since there was no case, no body, no investigation. "I did wonder if Marshall had invested in the development where you tried to rent an apartment."

"Had he?"

"No, but he knows the men behind the project. But that's not against the law."

She met his gaze again. He swore she had the bluest eyes he'd ever seen. "You know he did it, don't you?"

He hadn't expected her to ask him point-blank, and for a moment, he was taken aback. Amy Sue Brand might be a little naive about how big-city politics worked, but she was no shrinking violet, and that worried him.

"All the evidence says otherwise," Russ said in answer.

She gave him a disgusted look. He thought for a moment that she would get up and leave, letting him find his own way back to his patrol SUV. Fortunately, their food came. He saw her making up her mind. Stay or go? She looked down at the burger and fries placed in front of her.

"Do you know how a person could get from Great Falls to Billings, murder a woman, and then get back to Great Falls quickly enough it would appear he'd never left?" she asked and picked up a French fry from her plate.

Staying, he thought with a hidden smile. He was glad, more than glad, and that worried him because he liked her. Both the chief and his partner had warned him about getting too involved.

"No, but it's an interesting problem, don't you think?"

She grinned at him. "You mean trying to figure out how a person could be in two places at the same time? Or simple math? When I checked the mileage between the two cities, there was no way he could have driven back and forth. He had to have flown, but there were no connecting flights that would have worked. So that meant—"

"—he flew by private plane."

She cocked her head at him, her eyes gleaming. "Sounds like we both came to the same conclusion."

"It's the only way he could have done it, because I've checked out his alibi. Jack Marshall was at the conference in Great Falls. I know he flew there on Thursday and back on Sunday. He admitted to that, according to my chief."

"But that doesn't mean he didn't leave for a while. Does he have his pilot's license? Own a small jet, since that would be the fastest?"

"Jack Marshall does have his pilot's license and owns a small plane, but not a jet. Sorry to disappoint you."

Amy Sue shook her head. "I figure Jack Marshall is the kind of man that he knows someone with a jet who would have been happy to fly him back and forth—even in the middle of the conference."

"No one has come forward," Russ said.

"Because no one knows about the murder accusation against him, do they? The person has no reason to come forward with information."

Clearly, she'd given this a lot of thought. "That's true, and unfortunately, I don't have probable cause so I can't get a warrant from a judge to check the private flights and passengers to see how he could have committed murder before returning to Great Falls."

"No body, no evidence other than that pesky eyewitness," she said with a shake of her head. "You're no longer saying alleged murder," she said, smiling.

Russ shook his head but couldn't help smiling. He'd said more than he knew he should have, but he wanted to be as honest as he could with her. She was right about one thing. She had no business investigating Jack Marshall. Neither did he. "I believe you saw a murder but what we need is—"

"A body."

"That would definitely move things along," he said. "But just a missing person matching the description you provided might be enough to get the department to investigate. Right now, there is no case, no body, no evidence, no investigation."

"Except ours," she said, and took a bite of her meal.

"That's what worries me. If we're right, you're rattling the cage of a killer."

She chewed for a moment, swallowed and asked, "Could you lose your job if anyone finds out what you're doing?"

"I'm not worried about that as much as I'm worried Marshall will get wind of what we're doing and come after you. After all, you're the eyewitness. Without you..."

Russ saw her shudder at his words. From the beginning she'd known how dangerous it was. "I'd feel so much better if you went back to the ranch and—"

"I'm not safe there anymore either," she said. "I'm not

safe anywhere. That's why I'm here in Billings. I won't be safe until Jack Marshall is behind bars."

"What if that doesn't happen?" he had to ask.

"Knowing the lengths Jack Marshall went to to cover up his crime? From the moment I saw him coming out of the ranch road, I've felt it was just a matter of time before he gets rid of me. I'm a loose end and from what I can tell, he doesn't like loose ends. So my life was in jeopardy the moment I saw him stab that woman to death. There is no going back from that."

Russ understood, that's why he was worried about her. Marshall had too much power as a prominent figure in this city, this state, and a far reach in politics. Even behind bars, the man would be dangerous.

He feared she was right. She wasn't safe anywhere. Even if she stopped investigating the murder right now, she would still be a risk for Marshall. "We need someone to report this woman missing and soon."

But even with that, he wasn't sure it would be easy to tie her to Marshall. The man was too careful. Yet he had to believe there was a way to bring Marshall to justice, because he could see how much Amy Sue needed to believe it.

Smiling, he reached over and took her hand. "We're going to get him. I'm not giving up, and I can see that you aren't either."

She shook her head. "I know you don't like me rattling his cage—."

"No, I don't. He might decide to take care of you sooner than later."

"Well, if he does, I know you'll catch him."

He squeezed her hand. "I don't even want to think

about anything happening to you." Color rose in her cheeks. He quickly let go of her hand, reminding himself that he was the detective, and she was the eyewitness. "Please, Amy Sue, be careful. You're still staying at the hotel, right?" She nodded. "Don't ever let him get you alone."

Chapter Nine

Jack had desperately wanted to leave the office after the detective's surprise visit earlier, but after closing his blinds, he'd made himself stay. Taking off right away would make him look guilty, and the last thing he wanted to do was be followed. The gall of that detective coming to his business to question him. He couldn't believe that this hadn't blown over by now.

More concerning was Amy Sue Brand. He'd really thought that after his visit to the Brand ranch, his so-called eyewitness would have been scared off. She knew who she was dealing with and what he was capable of, so why wasn't she backing off? The woman definitely had to be deranged. She was certainly irrational to go to the police with that ridiculous story.

He'd silently cursed himself for going out to the ranch. But he couldn't help being curious. Also, he needed to know who and what he was dealing with. He'd thought he could scare her into changing her accusation.

Instead, that had been yet another mistake and now he had a police detective questioning him yet again. Fool-ish, foolish, he admonished. He'd tried to calm down and think. He'd been so sure nothing would come of this. It never should have gotten this out of control.

Amy Sue Brand had changed everything. The moment he saw her standing in that halo of light behind that adjacent building that night, he knew that she'd seen everything. He'd thought he was still safe, that he just needed to not overreact. He'd told himself he could fix this, he would fix this. And he thought he had, but that one detective wasn't letting it go.

He picked up his phone and called his good friend, Milt. "Chief," he said. "Hope your day is going better than mine."

"What's wrong, Jack?" Milt said. "Car sales down?" The chief laughed.

"Actually, they are, but I can still afford those cigars that you like," he joked back. "No, it's this ridiculous woman's story about me."

"Don't worry about that. We aren't taking it seriously, Jack."

"Maybe you aren't, but your detective was here just a few minutes ago giving me a hard time."

"My detective?"

"Tate."

"Oh, him. He's new and trying to make a name for himself. I'll take care of it."

"Thanks, Milt. It just looks bad to have cops coming and going here at work over some nonsense." The chief agreed. "We're going to have to go fishing up at Fort Peck again soon. You heard about the new boat I have coming? Bring that other detective. Hanson? I like *him*."

As Jack disconnected, his smile disappeared. Maybe he'd taken care of the problem. But as he walked over to one of his office windows and peered out from behind the blinds, he feared it was only temporary.

From the window, he'd expected to see the detective hanging around. But to his shock he saw something even more upsetting. There was that damned ranch woman as if he'd conjured her up. She had been standing in his showroom pretending to look at the shiny new car sitting there.

She'd looked up as if sensing him watching her. His first impulse had been to storm out of his office and demand to know what she thought she was doing. Fortunately, he'd come to his senses and reminded himself that according to what he'd told the cops, he'd had no contact with the woman, had never laid eyes on her.

Dragging his gaze away, he'd paced, afraid she would come to his office to confront him. What would she do if she did? Make a scene? Start yelling that he was a murderer? Maybe that would be good. It would prove just how delusional she was as she was being dragged away by the cops.

He'd been trying to decide the best way to handle her, when he'd looked out through the corner of the blinds and was surprised to find her gone. He'd glanced around thinking she might be behind one of the cars, but then he'd spotted her walking to her SUV parked out front—with Detective Russell Tate.

His pulse had thundered in his ears, his hands clammy and perspiration dampening his shirt beneath his suit jacket.

What kind of game was this woman and the detective playing? He'd felt his ire rise quickly. Like most women, she had no idea who she was dealing with coming here to…what? Scare him? Warn him? He hated that she'd done both. He rued the night he'd first laid eyes on her. Even then he hadn't realized what a nightmare the woman was going to be—let alone the detective. At least him, Marshall could get rid of without any bloodshed.

He felt even more vulnerable. He'd thought nothing more would come of this, but now he knew different. He couldn't chance anything else coming to light that might put him on the detective's radar.

With dread, he realized that he needed to make sure that the cops couldn't connect him to a woman named Whitney Clark. There was only one way to make sure that didn't happen.

Whitney could never become a missing person.

A MY SUE'S IMPROMPTU lunch with Detective Tate had left her unsettled. She'd been so certain that first night at the police station that no one was going to investigate Jack Marshall. Detective Tate had been kind to her, much kinder than the other detective. Tate hadn't disregarded her story and treated her as if she were delusional, but had listened as if willing to accept that she'd seen something that night and wasn't just making it all up.

But as he'd pointed out at lunch, all of the evidence made Jack Marshall look innocent. The police couldn't prove that the car dealer was anywhere near Billings the night of the murder.

That the police didn't have any more evidence than Amy Sue had gathered was upsetting. But now she felt as if she had an ally in Detective Tate. He had to know how much that meant to her. She'd been glad when they'd talked as she drove him back to where he'd left his patrol SUV. She thought of the look in the detective's warm brown eyes when he told her about growing up outside of Roundup on a ranch. "You're a cowboy?"

"Through and through."

She liked that about him, but wondered why he'd become a cop. The question had felt too personal, just like the way she had caught him studying her had felt personal. The cowboy in him wasn't the only thing about him that she liked. Her reaction to Russell Tate was enough to scare her. She'd been here before, feeling something for a man she really didn't know. Maybe the detective was on her side, maybe not. Either way, she had to be careful around him. Right now she desperately needed an ally and didn't want to read anything more into his attention.

Pushing away thoughts of the cowboy cop, Amy Sue focused on what she had to do to prove Jack Marshall had killed a woman the night in question. She had to find evidence that destroyed his alibi. Online, she found the conference Marshall said he'd attended in Great Falls. All she needed was to locate someone who'd seen him leave the hotel. Then she'd have the evidence she needed.

As for how he'd gotten to Billings and back to Great Falls without anyone being the wiser, she and Detective Tate both agreed it was by plane. She liked her theory of a friend with a jet plane and was determined to dig deeper into that.

Driving would have taken him seven hours round trip and that didn't include committing murder and getting rid of the body. She'd also checked commercial flights. None of them would have worked, plus there would be a record to show he'd left the conference.

But he could have taken a small private jet and made

the trip in less than an hour. The return flight would be about the same. Even if it had taken him an hour to get the woman to the house, he would have only been gone a little over three hours. He wouldn't have been missed at a large conference.

Amy Sue knew that she needed more information about Jack Marshall. What she couldn't find online, she'd have to get at his car dealership. She called to make an appointment with the service department.

When told that they couldn't get her in for a couple of weeks, she explained that she was from out of town. Couldn't they just take a quick look at it?

She agreed to bring it in the next morning first thing and they'd see what they could find.

RUSS FELT MORE worried about Amy Sue's safety after their lunch. The woman had put together a lot of the same theories he had about how Marshall could have been in two places at one time and committed what the man must have thought would be the perfect murder. That Amy Sue had figured out at least part of how it had been done made her more dangerous than even Jack Marshall knew.

Nor had Russ been able to talk her into going back home and giving up this plan of hers. True, she might not be safe anywhere, but when she didn't back off this crusade of hers, Jack Marshall was going to start throwing his weight around. He had the clout and the friendships even in the police department to have her arrested for harassing him. Worse, he might decide it was time to get rid of her for good. If so, it wouldn't be a stabbing, but an accident that wouldn't make him look more guilty than he already did. Russ wouldn't put anything past the man.

That he'd made up his mind about Marshall had him second-guessing becoming a detective. There was no evidence against the man. In fact, he found himself wishing that he could believe Amy Sue was wrong about who she'd seen murder that woman. Maybe Jack Marshall was innocent and therefore not dangerous.

But he did believe Amy Sue saw Marshall murder a woman—just as she'd seen the man on her ranch threatening her. Which meant she was also right about there not being any way to go back. It was why Russ would continue jeopardizing his job, because he couldn't back off, either.

What bothered him was the other reason he didn't want to quit. There was something about this woman that made him want more than anything to be her hero. He wanted to save her and put the bad guy in jail. It wasn't exactly why he'd worked to become a police detective, but then he'd never met a woman quite like Amy Sue Brand.

Getting involved with her, though, wasn't part of the job, he reminded himself. Lunch had probably been a bad idea, but he'd had to keep her from confronting Marshall—at least temporarily. Also he had wanted to know how intent she was in bringing the killer to justice. Now he knew.

There was no stopping either of them. He was already involved for the right reasons and maybe for one wrong one. He liked her, admired her for not going home and hiding under her bed. She wanted justice as badly as he did. They were both risking a lot, but with him, it was only his job. With Amy Sue, it was her life.

Watch yourself, he warned himself. "I'm going to do

everything I can to find out the truth about that night," he had told Amy Sue before they'd parted company. Against all odds, he believed she had seen Jack Marshall commit murder. More than ever, he wanted to bring the man to justice.

But the moment he walked into the police department, his partner called him over. "The chief wants to see you," Hanson said, adding under his breath, "I warned you."

Russ didn't have to ask what it was about as he made his way to the chief's office, tapped on the door and heard a grunt of reply for him to enter. Opening the door, he stepped in.

"Detective Tate," the chief of police said without looking up and motioned him into a chair in front of his desk. It wasn't until Russ had taken a chair that the man finally looked up. "I understand you're still investigating the man I told you not to even mention in my office."

There was only one answer to that question. "Yes."

"Why would you do that when there is no case?"

"There was an eyewitness, sir."

The chief leaned back in his chair, pinning him with a warning look. "There is no case because Jack Marshall was out of town and there was no evidence of a murder. The end. What about that don't you understand?"

"The eyewitness was very credible, sir," Russ said. "I believe she saw a murder."

"You're new here, Tate. I've done my best to cut you some slack," the man said as if finding it hard to spit out the words. "The department is not investigating Mr. Marshall. Period."

"I know he's a friend of yours but—"

The chief was on his feet, his big hands slamming

down on the papers on his desk as he lunged forward. He bit off each word, his face reddening, spittle coming out of his mouth. "I'm going to pretend you never said that. If you want to stay a detective in this department, you will move on to something else to investigate. Is that understood, Tate?"

"Yes, sir."

"Now get the hell out of here," he said, and dropped back into his chair breathing hard.

Russ rose, nodded and walked out the door. The chief's glare was like a target on his back. He tried to rein in his own anger, his own determination. He became a lawman to catch bad guys, and damned if that wasn't what he was going to do. The chief refusing to even let them investigate further proved what he had feared the moment he'd heard Amy Sue's statement.

Jack Marshall had killed that woman.

It SHOULD HAVE been the perfect murder, Jack kept telling himself. That it had gone awry because of one five-foot-five blonde drove Jack to distraction. How was it possible that Amy Sue Brand just happened to be there? Some fool had rented her an unfinished apartment and taken her money. If he could get his hands on whoever had done that—

He pushed the thought away. He had enough problems with the cops continuing to ask questions because of that one small complication. The police hadn't made a connection between him and Whitney Clark. Nor were they going to unless someone filed a missing persons report on her with the cops and they discovered a connection between him and Whitney.

Which had him worrying that the woman could have left something incriminating behind in her rental house.

So far, the cops knew nothing about her, but he couldn't take the chance, the way things were going. Before there was an eyewitness, he hadn't given it a thought. But now he had reason to worry. Detective Russell Tate was still investigating the non-murder. Jack hadn't liked the way the cop had looked at him. Surely the detective didn't believe Amy Sue Brand. Then again, he'd just seen the two of them leave together.

As he planned his visit to the house Whitney rented in Laurel, he couldn't help thinking about the day he'd seen her standing beside her broken-down VW Bug. She'd been too young for him but so beautiful. She'd told him she was twenty-four. Turned out she was much older, but he hadn't known that until he went through her purse before he got rid of it and her.

She'd told him she came from a family with money and was getting her master's degree in psychology. She had only one friend in the area, an old college roommate, but otherwise no family and few friends. Instantly, he'd known that she was his kind of woman.

The day he'd seen her beside her VW on the highway with her thumb out, once he'd seen her, he'd wanted her. She was young and beautiful with long dark hair, big green eyes and a body that would stop traffic. He was lucky he spotted her before anyone else did and pulled over to help. He'd thought it would be a one-off.

She hadn't recognized him, and he found that quaint. In hindsight he now knew that she'd only pretended she didn't know who he was. He hadn't offered his name even when he asked if she could use a ride. She'd eyed the suit he was wearing and the luxury car he was driving and hopped right in. He should have seen the dollar signs gleaming in her eyes, but he was breathing in her sweet scent and trying hard not to look at the gap in the tight buttoned-up shirt barely covering her full breasts.

He'd driven her to a small house outside of Laurel and offered to have her car towed. She'd asked him in and inquired about a good cheap mechanic. He'd called one for her on her phone. When he finished, she said, "Thank you," and held out her hand. "Whitney Clark."

"Jack Marshall," he'd said, and she'd pretended the name hadn't registered. Within minutes, they were in her bed. He'd planned to drive away and not look back. But as he was leaving, she came to the door in only her bra and panties and, smiling, waved goodbye. She'd known he would be back, and she'd been right.

He glanced at his watch now. He'd waited as long as he dared to do this. Checking his rearview mirror to make sure he hadn't been followed, he took the Laurel exit. He couldn't help being paranoid after the cops had made him give them a statement. Were they watching him? He didn't think so, but he didn't trust Detective Tate, a new detective on the force. Tate didn't know how things worked in this city, the largest in Montana, Jack told himself. But the cop would learn if he crossed Jack Marshall, he thought.

Chapter Ten

Amy Sue spent the afternoon and evening tracking down more people who had attended the same conference as Jack Marshall. She'd fibbed and said she was doing a story on the conference. She found people opened up better if they thought she was writing an article for a business magazine.

Jack had done a presentation earlier in the day during the conference, but few people recalled seeing him later that afternoon. One man remembered him in the bar after lunch talking with another man. Unfortunately, he didn't know the other man's name and suggested she ask Jack since it had appeared to be animated conversation about flying.

Could that be the man Jack had gotten to fly him back and forth to Billings that afternoon? Probably not, she decided. He would have planned everything long before the conference, right?

Learning little except that the conference had been large and while many of the people remembered seeing Jack, they weren't sure when it was. No one could definitely say they saw him the evening of the murder. Again, she had produced no real evidence.

Discouraged, she got off the phone and went to the

airport, hoping to learn something more. The news there was worse. She couldn't get anyone to talk about the private planes or their owners, let alone tell her anything about Jack Marshall on the night of the murder.

Wondering if she should just give up and go home, she called her sister, who was finally out of court. "I think you might be right about me not being a detective," she said when Josie answered.

Her sister laughed. "You knew it wasn't going to be easy."

"I've found out a few things, figured out some others, but we need evidence. We need that woman's name. Better yet, Russ says, we need her body."

"That sounds so morbid."

"It is."

"We? I'm assuming that's you and Detective Tate? Am I sensing that the two of you are getting close?"

Josie had never asked about her love life because it had never been worth asking about. But after Amy Sue had chosen wrong and almost paid the ultimate price for it, her sister worried.

"You don't have to worry about the cowboy detective. It's not like that."

"I'm not. I'm worried about you," Josie said.

"You don't have to do that either. It's been strictly professional. His department frowns on him fraternizing with the eyewitness, even the one they don't believe. Tell me about the trial," she said hoping that was the end of that particular conversation.

"It's going well. I should be home next week. What about you?"

Amy Sue looked out at the day turning to dusk. "I

might be home by then, too." She hated the thought. It felt like giving up. But what more could she do?

"Just be careful, please."

"You know me."

"That's just it, I do," Josie said solemnly. "If you quit, it isn't because you gave up. This time it's because the odds were just too much against you."

THE SMALL HOUSE was outside of town on a dirt lane and not near any others. Jack was glad not to see anyone around as he pulled into the empty parking spot next to the house Whitney Clark had rented. One of the first things he had done after their last night together was report her car as abandoned and have it towed to the junkyard. If her one and only friend in the area came out here worried about her, he'd hoped she would think Whitney had left town.

It had been another example of Whitney not doing what he'd told her to. Instead of driving her car to the construction site, she'd taken an Uber. He'd already planned how he was going to get rid of her car that night. She'd complicated things for him, not to mention, she hadn't done what he'd specifically told her to do. An Uber driver had Whitney's information, but the only way that would become a problem was if her body was found or her photo made the news.

In retrospect, though, it had worked out better since Amy Sue Brand had surprised him by showing up unexpectedly. Still, too many things had gone wrong that night. Now he found himself questioning what else he might have missed. He'd been confident that no one knew about the two of them.

But he was beginning to realize that she might not have kept her promise to keep them secret given the things he'd learned after he killed her. Otherwise, he wouldn't be sitting in the nondescript, older trade-in he'd borrowed after-hours from the back car lot, dreading going into her rental.

He could no longer trust Whitney Clark. Or his luck. Had the universe been trying to warn him to abort his plans that night when an Uber pulled up and let her out? He'd been even angrier with her, even more determined to end it permanently. Was that why he hadn't seen the car parked in the dark on the other side of the apartment building?

Now, as he glanced around, he wondered if he was about to make another mistake. Her house was far enough away from anything and everyone that it should have been safe, but he'd only come here with her once. From then on, they met at hotels far from the city. He'd been so careful that this should have been over by now, he thought with growing frustration.

Even though he hadn't expected to see anyone around, he'd dressed in the older jogging clothes he kept at work. With the hood up, he could hide his head of thick dark curly hair and pale blue eyes—his two most distinguishing features.

"Quit stalling," he muttered to himself and, pulling on the gloves he'd brought, he used the key he'd taken from her key ring to open the front door. He was hit with the scent of her perfume as he turned on the overhead light.

He'd been surprised how neat and clean the small house had been the other time he was here, so wasn't surprised to find it looked the same. He'd liked that she had brightly colored pots of flowers and nice linens in her bath and on her bed. He now knew just how much she liked nice things and how far she'd go to get them.

Glancing around the small house, his fear was that she'd left something around like a diary or letters that could incriminate him. Fortunately, there weren't a lot of places to hide something, he thought as he removed a large garbage bag from his pocket. The plants were wilted. He'd leave those, taking only what he thought she would have grabbed before hitting the road.

He had no idea when her rent was due, but he wasn't taking any chances. He didn't think anyone would be surprised that she'd skipped out and left town without telling anyone—maybe especially her landlord.

In the bedroom, he took most of her clothes, leaving behind ones he'd never liked. He checked under the bed and in the closet but found nothing more of interest. As he turned to her bedside table, he opened the only drawer. Nothing exciting. As he started to close the drawer, he noticed the framed photos.

There was one of Whitney and an attractive redhead, the local friend? Whitney & Liz. Best Friends Forever! was written on it along with Love You Roomie. Whitney looked much younger than Liz. College roommates?

He stared at the photo before breaking the frame to see if she'd written anything on the back of the snapshot. Blank. Again he considered the snapshot, wondering just how good friends they still were and if Whitney had told Liz about him. Urging himself to hurry, he couldn't help thinking of the ways Whitney had deceived him. He'd told her he wasn't looking for a relationship. She'd said she felt the same way. She'd lied. Laura Whitney

Clark had even lied about her name he'd realized when he'd gone through her purse. Whitney was her middle name and she was thirty-two—not twenty-four like she'd claimed. She'd been in great shape and had certainly passed for much younger, but another lie.

What else had she lied about? He realized he was still holding the photo of her and her best friend. Of course she would have told Liz about them. The only question was did Liz also know his name?

Furiously, he threw the broken frame and the photo into the garbage bag. As he reached for the only other framed photo next to the bed, he froze.

It was a candid selfie of Whitney and a man. It appeared to have been shot at a hotel pool patio. In the photo, the man was checking his phone while she was smiling at her cell camera with him off to one side and slightly behind her. Clearly, she hadn't wanted him to know she'd taken the photo.

He let out a curse as he picked up the framed photograph. He'd told her absolutely no photos, and yet here they were together, and he was definitely recognizable as the man in the shot. When had she taken this? Not that it mattered. Another lie, another deceit. He smashed the frame against the nightstand, the glass shattering. He banged it a couple more times, then jerked out the photo and tore it to shreds, dumping all of it into his trash bag.

Trembling with rage at what a close call this had been, he reminded himself that he'd dodged the bullet by coming here. His instincts had been correct. If this best friend and former roomie became worried about Whitney and had seen this photo and gone to the cops, he would never get them off his back. His pulse pounded as he thought of how Whitney had manipulated him almost from the beginning with her lies.

Feeling a new urgency to cover his tracks, he moved quickly through the house, taking things he thought she would have taken if she'd been in a hurry to leave town. He broke some things, left drawers open and tossed clothes on the floor. Fortunately, the house was small and minimally furnished.

Slightly out of breath, he looked around, checking to make sure he hadn't forgotten anything. If her friend or her landlord came looking for her, they'd think that she'd left town for greener pastures. At least that was his hope.

He'd never asked Whitney anything about her friend, whom she'd mentioned a few times. What would have been the point since he'd known they weren't going to be together long? Now he realized that had been a mistake because he really wanted to know how to find the redhead if it became necessary. All he needed was another woman going to the cops with a wild story about him.

Worse, that would give the cops a name. Once the eyewitness identified Whitney from some photo Liz could supply, Amy Sue's story became a little too plausible.

He had to get this to end, he told himself as he stepped outside and loaded the full bag of Whitney's belongings into the trunk of the old car. He would dump it in a large trash container on the way back to Billings.

Leaving the house unlocked, he slid behind the wheel, hoping the old beater would start. Things in his life had gone as planned for so long, he had expected it to last—until the eyewitness the night of the murder. He'd always been so cautious. After that first time with Whitney when he'd given her a ride back to her place, he'd never returned until now. When he registered each time at a hotel far from Billings, he mentioned that his daughter would be joining him so he would need adjoining rooms. They never arrived or left together.

He had his routine down and it had always worked like a charm—until Whitney. Now he no longer trusted his good luck. What should have been the perfect murder had been anything but.

He realized he was sweating as he turned the key. With a sigh of relief, the car started, though it was running rough. He couldn't wait to get it back to the dealership, the bag in the back thrown in a dumpster on the way.

Still, he hesitated, feeling as if he'd forgotten something important.

That's when he realized what else was missing from the house other than Whitney. There'd been no sign of the student master's thesis she said she'd been working on, no paperwork in the house at all. The woman had lied about *everything*.

The thought rattled him. He was usually better at picking women who could be trusted and while not happy about it, had known the score and walked away without squawking.

As he drove down the road in the late-afternoon fading light, he felt an urgency to get away from Laurel and get rid of the trash in the trunk. He wanted to be rid of everything about Whitney Clark. He still couldn't believe how she'd fooled him. She was determined to marry a wealthy man no matter what she had to do. Once she'd set her eyes on him, there had been no turning back for either of them.

Liz Baker tried her friend's cell number, not all that surprised when it again went to voicemail. For the past two weeks she'd tried to convince herself that there was no reason for concern. It wasn't like she and Whitney talked every day. Sometimes they went for a week or two without talking, especially since they now lived so close.

But she was concerned because the last time she'd seen Whitney, her friend had told her something that had her more than a little worried. It wasn't anything new, Whitney's choice in men, she reminded herself. She and Whitney had been roommates at college. Before that, Liz had watched Whitney fall in love multiple times and always with the wrong man. Her friend would go into a downward spiral after the breakup and had eventually dropped out of college. Liz had hung in, graduated with degrees in history and art, both of which had turned out to be worthless. She'd gotten married to the first man who asked. That, too, had turned out badly since she was now recently divorced.

So could she really blame her friend for wanting more out of life by marrying better? The problem was Whitney hadn't found that wealthy man to give her that life—until recently. Before that Liz would get a late-night drunk call from her friend who was either crying or overly excited about someone she'd just met.

He's perfect. He has tons of money and he's crazy about me. That was usually the way the optimistic calls went. But soon after would come the late-night drunk calls with Whitney in tears because she'd been duped or dumped or both.

"Maybe your expectations aren't realistic," Liz would

tell her. "Does he have to be rich, handsome, successful and crazy about you and ready to get married?"

"I'm not like you," Whitney would say. "No offense, but I'm not going to settle." Liz had married Robert, who had his own roofing business. But when his business failed, they were quickly overwhelmed by debt and the marriage failed as well.

Liz knew she had no business advising anyone on relationships. "I just worry that you're always going to be disappointed. Did you ever consider your dream man might not exist?"

Whitney had scoffed at that. "I know that there's a man out there who can give me the amazing life I deserve. I just have to find him."

A few months ago, Whitney called to say she'd found the man of her dreams. She'd been over-the-moon excited. "He's perfect. He has his own business. He's very successful and handsome along with being rich."

"Who is this amazing man?" Liz had asked, trying not to sound skeptical.

"I'm dying to tell you, but we have to keep it hush-hush for now. He's in the middle of a really ugly divorce, but once the divorce goes through, we're going to get married." In the middle of an ugly divorce and yet ready to get married again right away? Liz must not have hidden her feelings quickly enough, because Whitney added, "He's having our house built for us to move into right after the wedding."

Building them a house? Getting married when the divorce goes through? *Oh, Whitney, what have you gotten yourself into this time*, was Liz's first thought. Was the man even getting a divorce, or was he lying like so many of the others had?

Liz had to bite her tongue. She didn't want to be the one who always tried to reason with her friend. Maybe it was true. Maybe Whitney had hit the jackpot. Liz certainly hadn't.

But she couldn't help feeling that this man was going to break her friend's heart. There was nothing Liz could say that wouldn't hurt Whitney, so she tried to be supportive. "He sounds like exactly what you've been looking for."

"He is. He said I'm going to love the house, and he can't wait to show it to me. It's still under construction, but he wants me to pick out everything so it's exactly the way I want it. He thinks I have a flair for decorating." She'd beamed. "He's promised to show me the house soon so I can start planning what I want to do. It's really happening, Liz. I know you've always thought I was being too picky and I was going to be disappointed."

"I stand corrected. I can't wait to meet him," she'd said, hoping this time Whitney really would get the man and the life she'd always dreamed possible.

"Once the divorce is over and we're in our new home, I'll have you and Robert or whoever you're with over for dinner. I can't wait for you to meet him."

"That sounds terrific," Liz had said, wondering if it would really happen. She definitely wouldn't be with Robert or maybe anyone for that matter. "You know I just want you to be happy."

"I am. I'm so lucky. Wait until you meet him. It's going to blow your mind."

Something in her tone had made Liz ask, "Is he someone I know?"

"I've probably already said too much," her friend had said with a laugh. "His wife is really awful. We have to keep our relationship quiet so she doesn't use it to get more of his money. She's one of *those*."

That was the last time Liz had spoken to her. She'd been worried ever since after what Whitney had—and hadn't—told her and then gone silent for the past two weeks. One thing was clear. The man was married and maybe in the middle of a bad divorce. It sounded like a dangerous place for Whitney to be. Liz had been expecting one of her friend's late-night drunk sobbing calls for several weeks now. But she also hadn't had one of her excited, my-life-is-going-to-be-amazing calls either.

Liz didn't have to be at work for several hours so she decided to drive to Laurel to the house Whitney had rented. Her friend wasn't answering her phone, which was unusual enough. She had a bad feeling she should have checked on her sooner.

On the drive from her own house south of Billings, she turned at the Laurel exit. Her hope was to find her friend planning her wedding or busy making decorating plans for her new house. What worried her that was this time Whitney might not be able to handle another broken heart. This time the disappointment might be too much for her. Liz knew firsthand what disappointment did to a person.

Russ couldn't get Amy Sue off his mind. Back at his desk, he pulled up the information she had given them about the person she'd rented the apartment from online. It was another piece of the puzzle and would prove that she was telling the truth if he could track it down. When he'd called the number she'd given him that night to verify what she'd told them about the rental, he'd left a message for the man to call him back. No one had and he'd dropped it, telling himself that it didn't really have anything to do with the murder that allegedly hadn't really happened.

But now he tried the number again and found that it was no longer in service. Well, that solved one mystery. When he'd called, he'd left his name and number at the police department. Amy Sue Brand was right, it had been a scam. Her money was gone, and he knew the department wasn't going to chase it down for her. But he thought he might look into it to see if it led anywhere.

What interested him was why the scammer had picked that specific address with the door around back and an entry pad and light next to it. Clearly, the person was familiar with the address. Had Amy Sue tried the code he'd given, she would have found out what Russ had. The numbers didn't work.

But why not give her a bogus address? It bothered him enough that he drove back to the construction site to find the crew still working on the apartment. Getting out of his patrol SUV, he flashed his badge to each employee he came across, looking for someone to react as he asked basic questions about the job.

He was beginning to think he was wrong until he spotted a young man with stringy dishwater-blond hair and worn work boots leaning on a shovel, visiting with several of his coworkers.

Russ flashed his badge and asked, "Did you work on

the apartment house over there?" The man nodded and glanced over as his coworkers moved off as if not wanting anything to do with whatever it was. "What can you tell me about the apartment in the back?"

The man shrugged and shook his head. "I need to get back to work."

"I just have a few more questions," Russ said. "Let's start with your name." He saw the man hesitate. "Better yet, show me some ID."

"I don't have it on me," he claimed, and looked toward a beat-up older model brown pickup parked at the curb.

"Is it in your vehicle?"

A quick headshake. "Rode with a friend." He shifted on his worn work boots. Russ could see that he was making him nervous. "What's this about?"

"Fraud." The man's eyes widened. "A woman thought she'd rented that apartment online a couple of weeks ago. I'm going to need you to come down to the police department to see if she recognizes your voice."

Russ was more than ready for what came next as the man slung the shovel at him and took off running. The detective was on him before he reached the open fields behind the new addition.

He tackled him, driving him to the ground. "You have the right to remain silent," he began as he cuffed him, then pulled out the man's wallet that was now sticking part way out of his sagging jeans. "Emery Olsen, let's go." He pulled him up from the ground and walked him toward his unmarked patrol SUV.

Emery was saying, "You can't prove I did anything."

Russ figured the young man was probably right. It would be hard to prove, especially if Emery had dumped the burner phone he'd no doubt used. But before this man walked, Russ had some questions he hoped to get answered.

"If you cooperate with my investigation, I'll see what I can do for you."

JACK COULDN'T BELIEVE the lies Whitney had told him. He was shaken and fuming with anger as he left her rental house. He hadn't gone far when he saw a car turn down the lane toward him. He had hoped to get in and out of here without anyone seeing him, but he'd lost track of time while inside the house.

He touched the brake but quickly realized there was nowhere to turn off as the car came toward him. He lowered the brim of his baseball cap and reached for his sunglasses when he realized he didn't have them.

The driver slowed as they approached each other on the narrow road. He was reminded of the road out of Amy Sue Brand's ranch. As they passed, he saw the redheaded woman behind the wheel out of the corner of his eye. It was Liz from the photo he'd taken from Whitney's bedside table of the two of them.

In his surprise at seeing the woman, he hadn't realized that he'd let up on the gas. Worse, he'd done a double-check long enough to see her surprised expression. *She'd recognized him.* Even if Whitney hadn't told her friend about him, the redhead had just put it together.

He swore, sped up as he tried to convince himself that it didn't matter. Once she went to the house, found the door unlocked and Whitney's belongings gone, she'd believe that things hadn't worked out and Whitney had left town.

That was the story he would stick to if she ever confronted him.

He tried to breathe. He'd been so shocked to see the redhead behind the wheel that he hadn't tried to get her license plate number. He still didn't have a last name. He cursed his bad luck. Why hadn't Whitney just taken the payoff he'd offered her and left town for real? Why did she have to threaten to ruin him? She'd said she would go to his wife, then the dealership and make a scene. Then she would post all the juicy details of their affair online.

Now he knew that she would have done all of those things—along with releasing at least one photograph she had of the two of them. She had known that she had him backed him up against the wall with enough ammunition to blow up his life unless he left his wife, got a divorce and married her.

She'd given him an ultimatum with only one way out.

He swore and kept driving, surreptitiously glancing in his rearview mirror. Liz had pulled into the parking spot next to Whitney's house. He couldn't wait around to see if she went inside. He just had to hope his plan worked better than his last one.

Cursing himself for ever getting involved with Whitney Clark, he drove onto the interstate and headed back toward Billings. Now her best friend was another loose end, and he didn't know the woman's last name. He had no idea how to find her because he'd gotten rid of Whitney, her purse and her phone. He'd seen no reason to keep anything of hers. Until now.

He should have at least checked Whitney's call history. Why hadn't he realized she might have a friend in the area who she confided in? Someone like an old college friend she called her best friend? Because Whitney had only mentioned her friend in passing. He'd gotten the impression she was too busy with her studies to socialize. Except there were no studies. But there was Liz.

He kept thinking about the woman's look of recognition. Had it been accusing? He now thought it had, which meant Whitney had told her about him. He'd questioned her and she'd sworn she hadn't told anyone, but now he knew what a liar she was.

Jack groaned at how badly he had handled all of this. He'd planned the perfect murder, but then Whitney had given him an ultimatum and forced him to move things more quickly. Still the construction site had been the perfect place to get rid of his problem until Amy Sue Brand had ruined that. He'd misjudged her, thinking he could scare her off. He'd been so sure he'd taken care of her, that she'd gotten the message and wouldn't be a problem anymore—right until Detective Russell Tate had stepped into his office to accuse him of not just visiting the woman's ranch, but threatening her?

Now he had to worry about Liz too, whoever she was?

His mind whirred. Liz wouldn't go to the cops or report her friend missing until she talked to him, would she? No, he decided. He would have to deal with her when she called or, worse, came into the dealership to confront him.

But maybe he could turn this to his advantage, he realized. He would tell her that he had gone out to Whitney's house because he was worried about her. He cared deeply about Whitney, but he and his wife had reconciled and were trying to make their marriage work. Whitney had taken it badly.

Once Whitney had settled down, they both thought it best if she left town. He'd given her money to make a fresh start somewhere else. But then he hadn't heard from her. He was relieved when he went to her house to find that she had packed up and left, though clearly still upset.

Jack thought he could sell that; after all, he was one hell of a salesman.

And if he couldn't convince Liz that her best friend had left town?

That would be her mistake.

Chapter Eleven

As Russ drove away from the jobsite and alleged murder scene with Emery locked in the back still handcuffed, the man began to talk.

"Look, what I did was stupid, okay?" he said. "My truck was broke down. I was desperate because I gotta have the truck to get to work."

"Are you trying to tell me this was the only time you did this?"

"It was, I swear. When my boss found out, I almost got fired. Now if I have to go to jail…"

Russ pulled into a vacant business's parking lot. "Maybe you can help me with another case I'm working on. Do you know a man named Jack Marshall?"

"The car guy from TV?"

"Have you ever seen him at your jobsite?" Russ asked.

"A few times."

"He friends with the property owner?"

"He's friends with everybody, going around glad-handing everyone like he owns the town," Emery said.

"Did he talk to someone about buying one of the houses?"

"I saw the boss take him into one."

"The one next to the apartment you rented online?"

Emery frowned. "Yeah, that one."

"What is your boss's name?" He took down the name Frank Johnstone and his phone number. "I'll tell you what, Emery, I'm going to let you go. But I expect you to pay back the woman you duped. Fair enough? That's what I thought you'd say. I'll see that you get an address to send the money, even if you have to send partial payments for a while. Agreed?"

Emery had quickly agreed, so he'd taken him back to the jobsite and dropped him off.

"The crew is going to be curious. I'd appreciate it if the story you tell them doesn't involve Jack Marshall."

LIZ FELT SICK with worry and shaking with the shock of what she now knew as she sat in her car in front of Whitney's house. In her rearview mirror, she watched the older car she had passed disappear back up the road. That was him. She knew it based on all the hints Whitney had given her, and now she'd just seen Jack Marshall coming from Whitney's rental house. Add to that he was driving an old beater car wearing a baseball cap and a hoodie sweatshirt hoping no one would recognize him.

She groaned. Hadn't she known that her friend was in trouble? Jack Marshall was just the kind of man her friend would have set her sights on. Money, high profile and handsome. But why were they always married? According to Whitney he was getting a divorce, but Liz hadn't heard anything about that and figured Jack Marshall had lied. Whitney had wanted it to be real, all of it, so she had believed whatever the man told her.

But Liz suspected none of it had been true. Had Whitney found out? Is that why Liz hadn't heard from her?

She glanced at the empty space where Whitney usually parked, then at the house. No lights on inside. No sign of life. Her friend always left the light over the front door on where she never had to come home to the dark. Was it possible she'd moved into this new house her lover was supposedly building for her?

Doubtful, she thought, given what she'd just seen. Just as doubtful was that Whitney was somewhere waiting for "the man of her dreams" to return. Since she'd driven out here, Liz told herself that she might as well check the house. Getting out, she looked back up the road, glad to see no vehicle headed her way. She would make this quick and get home before dark. Like her friend, she didn't like coming home to an empty house with no lights on.

Now that she suspected Jack Marshall was the man Whitney had been in love with, Liz was even more terrified that something bad had happened to her friend.

She still had the spare key Whitney had given her, but as it turned out, she didn't need it. The door was partially open. Her heart pounded as she pushed it in, terrified of what she was about to find.

Russ found Frank Johnstone at the construction site where the alleged murder had taken place. He had to assume that anything he said to anyone about Jack Marshall was going to get back to Jack—and then his boss. Yet he'd become a detective to catch criminals, and that was exactly what he was trying to do.

"Mr. Johnstone," he said as he entered the small temporary office. "I'm Detective Tate investigating a possible homicide. I'm hoping you can help me."

The sixty-something stocky man behind a large desk motioned him in. "A homicide?"

"I need to know if Jack Marshall talked to you about buying one of your houses here."

Johnstone raised an eyebrow. "Not sure what that might have to do with a homicide, but yes, Jack did show some interest in a house."

"The one next to the apartments?" Russ asked, pointing out a window across the street. "Did he set up a time to look at it? Ask for a key?"

"Not really. He said it would be after work. I told him I'd leave the back door open."

"Do you happen to remember the date he planned to see it?" he asked, practically holding his breath as the man gave the date of the murder.

"I remember because I had an offer on the house the day before and told him if he wanted it, he'd have to make an offer soon," Johnstone said.

"Did he make an offer?"

"No, said it wasn't quite what he was looking for." The man shrugged. "I think he was looking for investment property. What's this about a homicide?"

"I'm afraid I can't say, but I appreciate your time."

"I hope I was able to help," Johnstone said.

"You were."

As he left, Russ knew that this, too, wasn't enough to get the chief to open an investigation. He needed more. He needed a body. He glanced toward the newest building coming up in the subdivision and recalled that it had been an empty hole in the ground the night of the murder. Now it would take quite a bit of excavation to dig up the concrete that had been poured looking for a body beneath it.

At every turn, he felt stymied. Bringing Jack Marshall to justice felt impossible. He feared he'd never be able to find hard evidence against the man.

JACK SWORE UNDER his breath as he walked into his showroom and saw Detective Tate waiting for him yet again. Obviously, Milt hadn't taken care of the problem.

"Mr. Marshall," the detective said, rising to greet him.

"Detective Tate," he said, ignoring the man's outstretched hand as he walked past him to open his office door. "I thought I made myself clear the last time you were here. I'm not talking to you without my attorney present."

"I just need a few minutes of your time," the detective said, following him into the office. "But I'd be happy to wait while you call your attorney."

Jack lowered himself into his big office chair in front of his massive desk and didn't offer the cop a seat. "A few minutes is actually more than I have."

"I'll be brief. Are you familiar with Briarwood Estates?"

He frowned and shook his head. "I don't understand what this—"

"It's the name of the new addition where the eyewitness claims she saw a murder. Do you have a financial connection to Frank Johnstone or Thomas Armstrong or any others involved in Briarwood Estates?"

Jack glared at the cop. "Even if I did, I don't see where it would be any of your business."

"I'm sorry, is that a yes or no?"

He took a deep breath and let it out slowly, warning himself to be helpful, not make this detective any more suspicious than he already was. "No, I have no financial interest in…what did you call it?"

"Briarwood Estates. What about the other investors? Do you know any of them?"

Jack sighed deeply. "Detective Tate, I know you're just doing your job, though I have to wonder why you are continuing to ask me these questions. As I understand it, there wasn't a murder, and as you know I was out of town all that weekend."

"Sorry, but you didn't answer my question."

"I know Frank Johnstone and probably some of the other investors," he snapped. "You seem to have forgotten who I am. I own the largest car dealership in the Northwest. I know a lot of people—many of them buy their vehicles from me because they do know me and have for years."

"Oh, I haven't forgotten who you are," the detective said with a chuckle.

"Well, I have work to do."

"Did you talk to Frank Johnstone about buying a house in the new subdivision?"

Jack stared at the detective. The man was relentless. "I have a beautiful home up by the rimrocks overlooking the city, Detective. I don't need another home."

"But you did talk to him about one of the houses."

"I might have thought about buying one as an investment. I really can't remember."

"So, Mr. Marshall, you're saying you don't remember taking someone to the subdivision the night of the alleged murder to show them a house next to the apartments?"

Jack got to his feet. "I don't have time for this nonsense. Unless you're going to arrest me…" He tried to make a joke out of it, but the cop didn't smile.

"That's all for now," Detective Tate said. "I think I have what I came for." With that, he turned and walked out.

Jack swore under his breath, hating that he'd lost his temper, hating even more that he was sweating. This damned detective just wouldn't quit. He picked up his phone to call Milt again to complain about being harassed by the cops, but found himself putting the phone down as he spotted something that stole his breath.

Chapter Twelve

Amy Sue Brand was back in his showroom talking with one of his oldest and most loyal employees. They had their heads together as if George Harper was filling her in on all his boss's secrets. Unfortunately, he suspected old George might know a few.

Jack tried to catch his breath. First walking in to find the cop waiting for him yet again. He felt as if he were stuck in a nightmare. Why wouldn't Whitney just die? He couldn't believe how his planning had gone so awry. But he'd covered his tracks, so how was it that the police were still asking questions? It galled him that he'd come into work to find Detective Tate waiting to see him at his office yet again. He'd thought that he'd more than satisfied the authorities' inquiries and found himself getting testy that this one particular cop was still bothering him.

He knew he had to hold it together, but he was losing his patience. He kept telling himself that the woman couldn't hurt him any more than she had, yet her determination had him losing his mind. Didn't she have something better to do?

"Is everything all right?" his wife had asked him this morning as he was getting ready for work.

"I'm fine," he'd snapped. "The commercial shoot is this morning. I always get a little nervous."

"That's not true at all," Christine teased. "The camera loves you, and you love being in front of it."

He had tried to laugh it off, but the worried look she'd given him warned him that his anxiety was starting to show. True, he had been running scared, but he thought he was holding things together well enough. He'd flashed his wife his famous smile and drew her in for a kiss.

Jack couldn't bear the thought of losing her. He needed her by his side, and not just for her family money or their heritage. Christine ran their private as well as social lives, making it look easy. He didn't kid himself that he wouldn't be where he was now in life without her. That's why he could never make a mistake like Whitney Clark again.

"Sorry, just a lot going on right now," he'd said. "But everything's fine."

A lie. Nothing was fine, and that was the problem. Cops crawling all over him, a damned eyewitness he needed to deal with and now Whitney's best friend Liz to worry about. He shook his head.

On top of that, sales were down right now, he reminded himself. It was why he had a big sale coming up and a huge advertising campaign. He needed to get his head into the game, but he found himself glancing around every morning when he walked into work, expecting to see Detective Tate, Amy Sue or Liz—or all three waiting in his office.

His phone buzzed. The film crew were waiting on him back in the media room to shoot his commercial. He looked out the glass around his office at the shine of the new cars in the showroom to where Amy Sue Brand was getting an earful from George.

As he reached for his cowboy hat, he told himself to play it cool. What was Amy Sue Brand doing back here? She was as relentless as that blamed detective.

Shoving his hat down on his head, he left his office and walked over to where she and George were standing next to a large, very expensive shiny new car on the showroom floor. It was exactly the kind of car a farm woman from Dry Gulch, Montana, wouldn't be interested in buying.

Over the years, he'd gotten where he could tell if a prospective customer was really in the market for a car—especially one of the expensive ones that sat on the showroom floor.

This woman wasn't here to buy a car. Nor had she ever purchased one from his dealership, which meant there was only one reason she was here.

"Looking for a car," Jack said cheerfully as he approached and shifted his gaze to her, his smile faltering. "Once you get behind the wheel, you won't be able to walk away from this one," he said as he ran his hand over the smooth surface of the hood. "She's beautiful, isn't she? Too bad I don't have time to take you for a test drive."

"Nice car, but I'm not shopping for a new car, Mr. Marshall. George and I were just visiting. He said he's your oldest employee, been here since you took over the dealership. That's a long relationship. You can learn a lot about a man in that length of time." She was smiling and so was George. "Bet he knows all your secrets." She chuckled, and George joined her, unaware of who she was or how dangerous this woman was. "I wasn't surprised to hear that you have your pilot's license and your own private plane, but no small jet although you've been shopping for one. I'm shocked you have any time to use it as busy as you are."

Jack managed to chuckle and smile even though he was fuming inside, his blood thundering in his ears. How dare George tell this woman anything about him, not that it was a secret. George was probably just making conversation, thinking she was doing the same.

But enough was enough. He had to end this right now. His gaze shifted to the older man. "George, sorry to break this up, but I need you to see to that trade-in that just arrived out back. I'll take care of this young woman."

George nodded and quickly hurried off, leaving him alone with Amy Sue. The moment the older man was gone, Jack turned on her. "I don't know what you think you're doing but—"

"Just waiting for my car to be serviced," she said. "Your service manager seems nice and well meaning. Don't take it out on him just because he's been with you for a long time and is proud of your success. He still thinks you're a nice guy."

"I see what you're doing," Jack said, keeping his voice low. He looked away from her, fighting to rein in his temper. He'd built this business, this life, all of it because he could be calm, cool and collected when he needed to. He needed to right now as he stepped closer to her. "You should leave, and if you're smart you won't come back," he whispered.

The front door opened on a gust of wind. Stepping back from the petite blonde, he smiled and said, "Let me call the service department. I bet your car is ready." With that he turned and walked away before he did something he would regret. Once he had the service manager on the line, he said, "Amy Sue Brand's car. Get it ready and get her off the lot."

Amy Sue tried to still the way her insides quaked, her heart a pounding drumbeat of both fear and exhilaration as the man walked away. It was the first time she'd stood close to a murderer, let alone spoken to him the way she had. The man had an air about him of importance and power that she knew wasn't just air. She didn't have any doubt that he could crush her in all kinds of ways—not to mention kill her as he had the woman the night of the murder. It was no wonder he terrified her.

She had looked into those intense pale blue eyes of his and felt as if she were locking gazes with the devil. How could he be so handsome, so rich, so powerful and yet so evil, that others didn't see past his smile? He had everything, yet he didn't, or he wouldn't have a mistress, let alone kill her. She reminded herself that his need for a mistress was his weakness, his Achilles' heel, his fatal flaw. If it didn't bring him down, then she would have to.

As her pulse slowed, she told herself that Jack Marshall wasn't all-powerful. He hadn't committed the perfect murder, and he wasn't going to get away with it. She had to believe that. Otherwise, what was she doing other than merely upsetting him? How could she bring down the man?

She considered going to his wife, but it was the last thing she wanted to do. What did she think? That by destroying his marriage she could make him confess what he'd done?

No, what she had to do was find evidence to force the police to act.

It angered her that when he'd spotted her from behind the glass of his office window, he'd recognized her at once, which was damning enough since he'd lied to Detective Tate saying he'd never laid eyes on her.

He'd been startled to see her, maybe even shocked to find her standing in his showroom talking to one of his salesmen. It had definitely upset him. He had no longer looked quite so arrogant. She'd scared him. It was small comfort.

So what had been her plan? She had wanted to shake him up. She'd also wanted him to know she was coming for him. But when she'd stood toe to toe with him and looked into his ice-chip-blue eyes, a chill had rattled through her as she was reminded of just how dangerous this man was. She'd done her best to cover her fear, but knew she'd failed when he'd quirked a mocking smile. He thought he could use her fear against her.

That was the worst part. Jack Marshall wasn't worried about her doing real harm to him. This was a man who believed he was untouchable. Just as he knew he was even better-looking up close than on television. Who better than an arrogant con man when it came to selling especially women anything he had to offer?

She watched him go toward the back of the building, ignoring her, thinking he had gotten the last word. She tried to find satisfaction in the fact that Jack had recognized her, which meant she'd caught him in another lie. It made him look guilty since he'd told the police he hadn't been on her ranch, didn't know her name or where she lived, and wouldn't know her if he saw her. But she knew that if she went to them with this they'd laugh in her face.

She felt her anger bubble up even more. He'd apparently believed that he'd scared her enough out at the ranch that she wouldn't dare talk to the police again, let alone show up at his car dealership. Scaring her had only had the opposite effect. As much as he terrified her, she wasn't going to let him get away with what he'd done.

After a moment to catch her breath and stop shaking inside, she followed him and the sound of voices down the hallway. They'd left the door to the room open. As she peered in, she saw Jack step up onto a small stage decorated for spring with pots of different colored tulips. A mural of a country road cutting through new green grass under a Montana blue sky hung on the wall behind him.

Jack took his place, adjusting his cowboy hat. He appeared nervous. Seeing her definitely had upset him. "Give me a moment," he said to the cameraman. She watched him apparently shake it off.

After a moment, he looked up at the camera, then gave his spiel in a folksy Western accent nothing like the man she'd just met. Today, though, it seemed to lack his usual exuberance.

"Let's do a couple more takes," he told the cameraman, and looked past the lights to see her standing in the doorway. Eyes widening, a thunderstorm of an expression filled his suddenly flushed face. He kicked over one of the pots of flowers as he bound off the stage and strode toward her as if he wanted to kill her.

She hadn't expected him to move so quickly. Her breath caught. Her feet felt rooted to the floor. She started to raise a hand to protect herself when Jack grabbed the edge of the door and slammed it in her face. She heard him lock it. On the other side of the door, she heard him snap at the cameraman, "I'm ready now. Let's just get this over with."

When she could breathe again, she turned and walked down the hall. She'd half expected him to chase her out to her car. She saw George look at her almost apologetically as she pushed open the large glass doors and stepped out into the cool June day. She sucked in air as he walked toward her.

"Your vehicle is ready," George said, and handed her the keys. "I brought it right around for you." He pointed to her SUV parked out front. "Have a nice day."

She thanked him before he could hurry away. She'd gotten a little information out of him, less out of the service manager. She wondered if anyone really knew the real Jack Marshall. Unlocking her car, she slid behind the wheel and looked back at the showroom.

The sun glared off the glass front of the building. She didn't see Jack. She'd seen enough of him today, and she figured he felt the same way. However, several of his salespeople had come outside and were watching her with naked curiosity.

As she started the engine, she thought of her sister's warnings—and Detective Russell Tate's as well. She'd poked the bear. She wondered what he would do now, if anything.

He couldn't call the cops since she hadn't done anything wrong. How could he explain that he'd recognized the woman who'd made the false statement about him? He couldn't. There was no reason for Jack to even know who she was unless he saw her the night he killed his mistress. Not to mention the day he'd passed her on the ranch road and pretended to shoot her. She feared next time he pointed a gun at her, it would be the real thing.

But then again, she thought, remembering the night of the murder, Jack Marshall seemed to like knives.

Chapter Thirteen

Liz told herself not to do anything impulsive. She needed time to think as she drove toward Billings. The last thing she should do was anything rash. She hadn't slept well after seeing Jack Marshall coming from Whitney's rented house. Her brain kept replaying it until the wee hours of the morning when she'd finally dozed off, exhausted. Did Jack Marshall really think he'd fooled her with his beat-up car, his hoodie, his baseball cap?

She scoffed. He might be one of the most recognizable men in the county, maybe the state because of his television commercials. Even without them, the man stood out. As if he didn't know how handsome he was. He'd used that and his apparent charm to sell cars for years. He was everything Whitney had dreamed of.

One late night after talking about the man she planned to marry, Whitney had opened up about her childhood. "You don't know what it's like to be dirt poor," her roommate had said from the darkness of their shared college room. While Liz had been half asleep, something about Whitney's tone had made her stir herself fully awake to listen. She'd suspected her roommate's life hadn't been as normal as she'd wanted everyone at college to believe.

"Living in an abandoned house, going to school smelling like a skunk because one had gotten in through a hole in the wall the night before." Her voice lowered. "The way the other kids walked past me as if I didn't exist or made fun of me behind my back because of my ill-fitting hand-me-down clothes. There wasn't water in the house. I bathed in the creek out back except in the winter." Her voice faltered. "There were these jars of canned food in the basement we were afraid to eat but sometimes I was so hungry..." Whitney had fallen silent.

Liz had lain perfectly still, feeling her friend's pain. She'd known girls at school who came from less fortunate families. But there was one that filled her full of shame at the memory of how she'd avoided the girl because of her homemade ill-fitting clothes, her dirty hair and the smell. Kids at school said her family didn't have running water.

Listening to her roommate's confession, Liz hadn't moved, hardly breathed until she was sure Whitney had fallen asleep. The next morning, she'd pretended she'd been sound asleep and had heard nothing, again ashamed of herself. But while she hadn't known what to say, Whitney's revelation had left its mark on her. While she'd hoped her friend would find the fairy-tale life she yearned for, Liz had feared it would always elude her and eventually destroy her.

Was it Whitney's neediness or her beauty that had attracted Jack Marshall to her friend? Not that it mattered, she thought as she turned off the interstate and headed for the man's car dealership. He'd done what so many other men had. Played to Whitney's need for that perfect life, making promises he never planned to keep, lying until he was finished with her and then discarding her like yesterday's trash.

Even as she told herself it was a bad idea, she pulled into the parking lot of Jack Marshall Auto determined to find out what this man had done to her and where Whitney had gone.

JACK WAS STILL fuming even after he finally got a decent take for the commercial. He couldn't wait to call the chief of police. He was through fooling with Amy Sue Brand. Once behind his desk, he made the call only to be told that the chief was out of the office. He asked for Detective Hanson, but was told by a dispatcher that he was being put through to Detective Tate since Hanson was also out of the office.

"Wait," he said, trying to stop her. "I don't want to talk to Tate."

"Sorry, but you've got me anyway," the detective said. "What can I do for you, Mr. Marshall?"

Jack groaned and thought about hanging up. "When is Detective Hanson going to be in?"

"Not sure. He was called away on a family emergency. Maybe I can help you."

"I'm being harassed, and I want her stopped," Jack said with a curse.

"Her?"

"That Brand bitc—woman. This is the second time I've seen her in my showroom, but today—"

"Wait, I thought you've never laid eyes on the woman. Are you sure it was Amy Sue Brand? Oh, that's right, you saw her the day previously to when she filed a report that you came to her ranch and made a point of pretending to shoot her?" Tate said. "You must have recognized her then since you were on her property."

He bit back a curse. Hadn't he known this was a mistake talking to Tate? "Why if I had threatened her on her ranch would she show up at my car dealership to harass me?"

"That's a good question, since wasn't the idea to scare her off?"

"Let's not play games, Detective. Are you going to do something about her or not?" he snapped. "Or am I going to have to do something about you?"

"You aren't threatening an officer of the law again, are you, Mr. Marshall?"

Jack gripped the phone. This cop was going down. He bit off each word. "This woman is after me. She's trying to defame me. She'll say anything to make me look bad."

"Why would she do that?" Tate asked.

"How should I know? I'm a public figure. It wouldn't be the first time someone was jealous of my success."

"A woman who runs a ranch in Dry Creek miles from here?" the detective asked.

"I don't know what her problem is, but she won't leave me alone."

"What would you like me to do about it?" Tate asked.

He tried to hold in his anger, but it bubbled up. He could feel the heat of it burning his face, roiling his stomach. He sometimes lost control when he got this furious, and he made mistakes. "Make her stop. Isn't that what I pay your wages for?"

"I'd be happy to speak to her on your behalf," the detective said.

"Speak to her? Lock her up! She's dangerous! Next

time she might come on my property with a gun and kill me."

"Do you want to take out a restraining order on her?" Tate asked.

Wouldn't the detective just love it if that got out about the woman who accused him of murder. He gripped the phone so hard he thought it would break. "Never mind. I'll take care of it myself."

"I wouldn't suggest—"

But that's all he heard before he threw his phone across the room.

Russ didn't need his partner around to tell him that he was walking on dangerously thin ice. Jack Marshall was off-limits. The chief had made that clear, and he'd watched the way Detective Hanson was with Marshall. Careful. Almost coddling the businessman.

It made him sick. He could barely contain his contempt for Jack Marshall no matter how hard he tried. He knew it was going to cost him his job. But he desperately wanted to see the man behind bars before anyone else got hurt.

He immediately thought of Amy Sue. She wasn't going to stop trying to prove the man was a murderer. He raked a hand through his hair. It wasn't as if she didn't know who she was dealing with. The woman was stubborn as some of the horses Russ broke on the ranch, he thought with a smile.

He couldn't help himself. He admired the hell out of her, but he feared they were both making a mistake going after Jack Marshall. With him, it would mean his job. With Amy Sue, she was playing Russian roulette with her life.

It was late, long past quitting time. Russ rubbed his temples as he leaned back from his computer. The office was nearly empty this time of the night. Only a few officers on duty, most of them out patrolling. What was he still doing here?

He sat forward again and kept looking for something in Jack Marshall's past. A red flag of some kind. He couldn't shake the feeling that if Jack Marshall killed a woman that night and Amy Sue witnessed it, then that wasn't his first time. It was too well planned. The alibi, getting rid of the body, making sure there was not even a sign of a confrontation wasn't luck. It was due to planning and practice. It nagged at Russ. Jack Marshall had killed before and gotten away with it.

Except Russ refused to believe there was a perfect murder. Amy Sue accidentally being at the scene and witnessing the murder proved that. This couldn't have been his first brush with the law. If there was evidence that was missing in his past, Russ was determined to find it.

AMY SUE SAT in her car, engine running, in front of Jack Marshall Auto, unsure what—if anything—to do next. What had she accomplished by all of this? Nothing. Just how far was she willing to push this man knowing what he was capable of doing?

Pondering that question, she noticed a woman with short red hair get out of her older-model vehicle. The redhead stood for a moment as if as unsure as Amy Sue felt, except this woman was nervous, almost scared. For a moment, the redhead looked as if she was going to climb back into her car and drive away.

But apparently a decision made, she straightened and stalked toward the showroom door, hitching up the strap of her large purse as she went. Amy Sue watched her, curious. The woman didn't appear to be here to buy a new car. She seemed jumpy and tentative as she pushed open the door and entered the building.

Something about the woman's behavior had Amy Sue opening her door and following her. At the entrance, she hesitated, then slipped in, determined not to see Jack Marshall again if she could help it. Worse, she didn't want him to see her.

When she spotted the redhead marching toward Marshall's office, she wondered if she could be another of the mistresses. She definitely seemed upset as she approached the office's open door and came to an abrupt halt.

Amy Sue moved so she could see past the redhead into the fairly large room. Marshall was at his huge desk. He hadn't seen the woman. Or at least he hadn't reacted to her. He seemed to be engrossed in the paperwork on his desk.

"Jack Marshall?" The woman's voice broke.

When he looked in the redhead's direction, Amy Sue stepped back out of sight but not before she'd seen his surprised expression. Marshall knew her, and he wasn't happy to see her.

The moment the redhead stepped a few feet into the office, blocking Marshall's view past her, Amy Sue quickly moved to the side of the office door without all the windows so she could hear what was being said without being seen.

She heard him say, "Can I help you?" and the redhead answered, "I'm here about Whitney Clark."

"I'm sorry, I don't know anyone by that name," the car dealer said.

The woman's next words were so quiet that Amy Sue barely made them out. "I know about the two of you."

"Like I said, I don't know—"

"Please, I need to find her and make sure she's all right. If you can just tell me where she is. Is she at the house you bought her?" He started to say something, but she stopped him with, "Don't lie. I know about the two of you."

Marshall was on his feet, moving to step past her as if to close the door. "You're mistaken, but please come in and have a seat."

Before he reached the door, the redhead turned as if to leave and blocking him from closing her in. She turned back so quickly he almost crashed into her. This time when the woman spoke there was nothing timid about her tone. "I know you lied to her about the divorce and probably everything else, but you can't lie to me. I know. If I don't hear from her soon, I'm going to the police." With that, she walked out, looking unsteady on her feet.

With a loud crack, Marshall grabbed the door and slammed it hard. Amy Sue stood frozen for a few seconds, shocked by what she'd heard, before she hurriedly followed the redhead out of the building and into the parking lot. Her mind was whirling. Was Whitney Clark who she thought it was?

She'd hoped to catch the redhead before she left, but

the woman was already behind the wheel and pulling away. Amy Sue rushed to her SUV and followed her, keeping the car in sight as they left the city.

If she was right, she now knew the name of the murdered woman.

Chapter Fourteen

Liz had known the man would lie, but she was still shocked that he would do it to her face. She'd never been so angry or upset or worried sick. She kept thinking of the rented house where Whitney had lived and the mess she'd found. She'd known her friend since college. There wasn't any way Whitney would have left such a mess. She liked things neat and organized, and she valued what little she had. The mess she'd found was Jack Marshall's doing. Liz was sure of it. She'd seen him leaving the house in that old car and dressed in disguise. But she'd had no problem recognizing him from his stupid commercials. Had he hoped that by making that mess, anyone looking for Whitney would think she left in a hurry?

By the time she drove to Park City, some miles from Billings, she had calmed down a little until she saw her ex-husband's pickup parked out in front of the house they'd shared. What was he doing here? She was in no mood for another argument with him, she thought as she got out of her car and headed for the door. She was too upset to even register the SUV that had turned down her street—or the car that turned behind it a few moments later.

"Robert?" Liz called as she pushed open the door, stepping in to kick off her shoes. *"Robert?"*

He came out of the kitchen looking sheepish. "I thought you didn't get off work until five. I got here early planning to wait for you."

"I took a sick day," she said, seeing what he had in his hand. "You out of beer at your trailer?" she asked, stepping past him hoping he'd at least left a bottle for her. "What are you doing here?" she demanded as she opened the refrigerator and began digging around inside it.

Before he had a chance to answer, there was a knock at the door. It startled them both. They shot each other a questioning gaze. The next knock was more insistent.

"Were you expecting someone?" her ex-husband asked suspiciously.

She shook her head. "Stay here." Turning away, she went to answer the door.

Jack Marshall felt as if he'd made yet another mistake. He'd stood in his office after the woman left, shaking with fury and something he hadn't recognized at first—fear. He'd recognized Liz when she appeared in his office doorway—and she'd seen it. He'd seen it register on her expression.

Whitney's friend had caught him flat-footed after the day he'd already had. He'd forgotten what he'd planned to say to her. But instead of admitting that he and Whitney Clark had an affair and split up, he'd gone with his standard line that came to his lips. He'd denied everything.

Liz hadn't been fooled. She knew about him and Whitney, and now all he'd done was give her more fuel to come after him.

He'd always been so careful, so meticulous, so in control of every situation. But now his life was out of control and getting worse.

With a shock, he realized that he also hadn't gotten Liz's last name. Without it, he wouldn't be able to find her. Just the thought had his body buzzing as his pulse drummed in his ears as if counting down the seconds while the woman was getting away.

He grabbed his keys and headed out the door. Normally he wouldn't have taken his own car, but nothing was normal anymore. As he cleared the front door, he caught sight of the redhead driving away. Rushing to his vehicle, he slid behind the wheel, cranked up the engine and followed her. White-knuckled, he tried to talk himself out of what he was planning to do.

His cell phone rang. Christine? She never called him at work unless it was important. Had that lunatic of a woman Amy Sue Brand gone to her with her outrageous story? He tried to calm down before he took the hands-free call.

"Christine, is everything all right?"

"You forgot, didn't you?" she chided cheerfully. "We were going to meet with the designer handling the remodel."

He swore silently as he tried to keep the old car Liz was driving in sight. He couldn't lose her as she headed south out of Billings. At least she hadn't headed straight for the police.

"I'm sorry, sweetheart. I got busy. You don't need my input anyway. It's sweet that you want it, but you're the one with the overall design in mind. I trust your good judgment."

She chuckled. "You're resorting to flattery? You aren't getting out of it that easily. You can see the overall concept when you get home. You aren't going to be late, are you?"

Was he? he wondered as Liz stayed on the interstate past Laurel. Where was she going? The next town was Park City, then Columbus. How far was he going to follow her?

Christine's voice filled the car. "You're going to be late, aren't you. It's all right. I know you have that big sale coming up. There is no hurry on these designs. Maybe at breakfast?"

"Definitely at breakfast," he said quickly, glad to be off the hook. "Thanks for understanding."

"I knew how ambitious you were when I married you. I love that about you. Wake me up if you get home before midnight, otherwise, I'll see you at breakfast."

He disconnected and breathed a sigh of relief when he saw Liz's blinker come on at Park City. He backed off just a little, since Park City was small enough he wasn't going to lose her.

It gave him time to think about what he was going to do about this latest threat.

AMY SUE HADN'T been far behind the redhead. Fortunately, traffic on the interstate had been light. She'd had no trouble keeping the maroon-colored vehicle in sight. The redhead hadn't driven fast, as if she, too, were mulling over her conversation with Marshall.

Following the woman down the interstate, Amy Sue had replayed what she'd overheard from the short conversation again and again.

Whitney Clark was missing. The redhead was worried about her friend who she believed had been having an affair with Jack Marshall. He'd denied it, nothing unusual about that, Amy Sue thought. The redhead had threatened to go to the police. But she hadn't gone straight to the police station.

All Amy Sue could think about was the woman she'd seen murdered. Was it possible Whitney Clark was the woman Jack Marshall had killed that night at the construction site?

There was only one way to find out, she told herself as she took the off-ramp at Park City behind three other vehicles and followed the redhead to a small subdivision. The woman turned into a driveway in front of a modest house and got out.

She'd watched the redhead go inside her house before pulling to the curb behind a pickup out front. As she got out, she wondered what she was going to say. What if the woman slammed the door in her face?

She hardly noticed a large dark car drive past on down the street and stop in front of another house. She expected to be turned away as she made her way to the front door and knocked. No answer. She knocked again a little harder, and the door opened, giving Amy Sue her first good look at the redhead. She was older than Amy Sue had originally thought. There were dark circles under her green eyes and, along with sadness, there was a wariness in her expression.

Amy Sue said the first words that came out of her mouth. "I saw Jack Marshall kill a woman two weeks ago and I think it might have been your friend Whitney Clark."

The woman looked as if she'd been slapped. She staggered back, grasping the door as if for support. "Is this some kind of bad joke?"

"I overheard you talking to Jack Marshall," Amy Sue said quickly, stepping closer as the woman started to close the door. Of course the redhead thought she was delusional. "I saw how upset you were in the parking lot earlier," she said rushing on. "I followed you here to find out if Whitney Clark was the woman I saw murdered."

"What's going on?" demanded a man's voice from deeper in the house. She heard heavy footfalls headed in her direction.

"It has nothing to do with you, Robert," the woman called as she turned to look over her shoulder as the gangly man appeared.

But Amy Sue only got a glimpse of him out of the corner of her eye. Her gaze was on a table in the entryway covered with an assortment of framed photographs, one in particular catching her eye.

"That's her," she exclaimed, tears burning her eyes. She'd thought she'd never know the woman's name, let alone prove she was dead. "That's the woman I saw Jack Marshall murder."

Chapter Fifteen

Christine felt her first real stab of worry. Something was wrong. She knew her husband. They'd been together twenty-two years. On any day, she could tell by his mood what was going on with him. He loved his work; nothing about it upset him. Car sales were up and down, but he'd never worried about that since money wasn't a problem.

There had been a few tense times over the years when he'd had to break off an affair that had gone sour and he'd seemed to take it hard. But those had been few and far between. In recent years, he'd let more time go between his affairs as if no longer needing other women as often. That had given her hope that the two of them might settle into a safer lifestyle.

The one thing she couldn't bear was him getting caught cheating. It would force her into a very uncomfortable position and destroy the life they'd built together.

She knew that Jack had just broken it off with some woman a few weeks ago. By now he should have been in great spirits. What he shouldn't have been doing was working late so much, as if he either hadn't been able to break it off or had already jumped into another extramarital relationship.

Neither was like him. But then again, he hadn't been

himself in all that time. Her cell rang. A friend calling to make a lunch date. Another friend calling about an appointment with a charity group. A text to confirm a nail appointment.

She declined the call and did something she seldom did while Jack was at work. She called him. It was late enough that he might be in his office alone since the dealership would have closed by now.

It rang four times before going to voicemail. She didn't leave a message. Where was her husband? Now she was really starting to worry. "Jack, what is going on?" She would never forgive him if he ruined everything.

Jack had lost sight of Liz. The call from his wife startled him along with irritating him. Did she really think he could care about this latest remodeling project of hers? He thought about picking up, but she would know he was in his car. She would be able to hear some of the interstate traffic noises even outside one of the more expensive cars he sold and drove any time he wanted.

Mostly, he was in no mood to try to hide the strain he was under right now so he let the call go to voicemail.

Ahead, he finally saw Liz's car in front of an SUV. Her blinker came on as she prepared to turn off at Park City. He felt a tidal wave of relief that he hadn't lost her as he followed a car length behind. When the SUV in front him pulled off the other way, he stayed behind Liz, taking his time, following at a distance for a few blocks until she parked in the drive of what he assumed was her house.

Driving on past, he parked up the street where he still had a clear view of the house in his side mirror. As he did, he saw the SUV that had been in front of him earlier. It pulled over in front of Liz's house behind an old faded red pickup parked at the curb.

His breath caught as he recognized the SUV—and driver, without needing to see Amy Sue Brand's face. He was just starting to ask himself what she was doing there when she got out and headed for the door Liz had disappeared through only moments before.

He swore, rubbing his forehead as he tried to make sense of what he was seeing. Amy Sue Brand knew Liz? That wasn't possible, was it? If so it had to be the world's largest coincidence.

A more logical conclusion would be that the two had met at the dealership. Amy Sue should have left before Liz had arrived. But if she hadn't, was there a chance the two had met out in the parking lot? Why else would the woman be here?

Otherwise, if by chance the two knew each other, then this felt like a conspiracy. He thought the cops might agree. He knew he could sell it to Milt because there still wasn't a body and, let's not forget, Jack had an alibi.

He wasn't naive. What could the two women have to talk about other than him as Amy Sue stood in the doorway. Jack tried to convince himself that there was nothing more he could do parked there on the street. He now knew where Liz lived in case he needed to come back.

As for Amy Sue… He found himself waiting for her to return to her vehicle. Going to her ranch, he had hoped to scare her enough that he didn't have to deal with her further. Clearly, she didn't scare easily. Maybe he hadn't been direct enough.

He wouldn't make that mistake tonight, he thought, as he decided to wait for her as long as it took.

Chapter Sixteen

Liz turned slowly, her legs already going weak before she saw the photograph the pretty blonde at her door was pointing to. "Whitney?"

"I was afraid I'd never know who she was," the young woman said. "After I overheard your conversation with Jack Marshall at the car dealership, I had to follow you. I had to find out if Whitney Clark was the woman I saw him murder."

"*What?* This is about that harebrained friend of yours, Whitney Clark?" Robert demanded. "This woman followed you home? Liz, what the hell is going on? If she saw Whitney get murdered, then why didn't she go to the police?"

"I did," the blonde cried. "They didn't believe me because he'd gotten rid of the body."

Liz felt her eyes fill with tears as the truth settled over her. The woman on her doorstep sounded unhinged, yet she had recognized Whitney. Hadn't Liz feared her friend was dead? Hadn't she known when she looked at Jack Marshall that he was lying? That he'd done something awful to Whitney, even worse than breaking her heart?

"Robert, leave. Now," she said, sounding a little frenetic, but knowing that if he didn't leave she might completely lose it. "Let me handle this."

He swore behind her. "I told you Whitney was trouble. You don't even know that this woman is telling the truth. It could be a scam, showing up at our door like this."

"*My* door," she corrected, and stepped back as she pushed the door open wider. "Go. If you don't, I won't be responsible for what I do."

He swore but pushed past her, shooting a dagger at the woman standing on the steps before stalking out to his pickup. Liz waited until the engine revved, and he took off in a cloud of diesel smoke before she cleared her throat and asked, "What did you say your name was?"

"Amy Sue Brand."

Her grip still on the door, she said, "I think you'd better come in. I'm Liz. Liz Baker, soon to be Liz Jones." She stepped back to let the pretty blonde enter, afraid of what the woman was going to tell her, but needing to hear it.

As she closed the front door, she thought of Jack Marshall sitting behind his big desk, lying through his teeth. "I can make coffee, but I think I'm going to need a drink," she said as she led the way into the kitchen and opened the high cupboard to fish around until she found the bottle she had hidden there from Robert.

"Vodka with diet cola?" she asked pulling down the bottle to turn to face the woman. Amy Sue nodded and took the seat at the table as Liz got the diet cola from the refrigerator and a tray of ice from the freezer.

"I'm sorry about your friend."

Liz had to choke back a sob so could only nod as she took out two glasses and began to fill them. When she finally found her voice again, she said, "Whitney and I were roommates at college and stayed friends despite our age differences. She was like my—" her voice broke "—little sister." She handed a glass to her surprise guest, pulled out a chair and sat down with her drink, cupping it in both hands. "I know Jack Marshall is a lying, cheating bastard, but a killer?"

Amy Sue took a sip of her drink. It was definitely different, but right now it offered a warmth that she needed. "I don't know how much you want to hear."

"All of it," Liz said, and took a gulp of her drink.

Amy Sue started at the beginning, telling her about renting the apartment online and realizing it was in a new subdivision that was still under construction outside of Billings.

"She told me her boyfriend was having a house built for her."

"That's what I thought when I saw the two of them. He appeared to be showing her the house. She was really excited."

Liz took another gulp of her drink, her eyes filling with tears. Amy Sue swallowed the lump in her throat and continued explaining how a light had come on in the house and she'd been relieved she wasn't alone when she'd seen the two of them.

"I'm not sure what happened, but something changed," she said. "The woman turned toward him and didn't look happy anymore. It all happened so fast."

Liz sobbed quietly as she finished telling her how she'd seen Jack Marshall stab Whitney and wrap her in the plastic he pulled down from the doorway.

"I stumbled back in shock and the light behind the apartment house came on. That's when he looked up and I recognized him. He looked directly at me. I saw the knife and the…blood."

They both fell silent, the only sound the soft clink of their ice cubes against their glasses. "You must have been terrified," Liz said.

"I ran to my car and took off for the police department. Unfortunately, by the time the police got to the house, Jack was gone. There was no body and no sign anything had happened, except the plastic sheeting that had been hanging over the door was gone."

"Why isn't he in jail?"

"He has what the police say is an airtight alibi. He swears he was at a conference in Great Falls and never left there all night." She stopped to take a sip of her drink, her throat dry. "The police didn't believe I even saw a murder, let alone that Jack Marshall was involved. They still don't believe me. That's why I chased you down. Without a body…"

Liz wiped her eyes and got up to refill her glass. She motioned to Amy Sue, who declined another one. "She told me about him, not his name but said he was somebody, but I never dreamed it would be Jack Marshall. Whitney was determined to marry a rich man. I can't tell you how many of them used her and then broke her heart." She sat back down and stared into her full glass for a moment before she spoke again.

"When I went out to the house she rented, I saw him leaving it, and I knew he was the one she'd been seeing. Whitney thought he was going to divorce his wife and marry her." She shook her head. "The rental house looked as if she'd packed up and left in a hurry, leaving a mess, which wasn't like Whitney. I knew something was horribly wrong, so I went to confront him. I'd hoped maybe he'd packed her up. Or that he'd put her up in the house she said he was buying her. I just wanted him to tell me where she was." She stopped to take a gulp of the drink. "He said he didn't know anyone by that name." She made a disgusted face and took another drink. "Lies. All lies, but I never thought that he would…kill her." She looked up. "If I go to the police and tell them…" Her face fell. "They aren't going to believe me either, are they?"

"There's no proof she is even dead, and with his alibi…"

"Poor Whitney. I wonder what he did with her." She began to cry quietly again before angrily wiping at her tears. "What can we do? He can't get away with this."

"Believe me, I feel the same way. That's why I've been here in Billings hoping to prove somehow that he did it. But unfortunately, he's a very powerful and dangerous man. At least now we have the name of the murdered woman and Whitney is missing, right? That is more than the police had before today. They can look into it, but if her body doesn't turn up—"

"They'll believe him, not us."

Amy Sue nodded. "I'm going to do everything I can to prove that he's lying. What you told me will help. I'm sure the detectives will want to talk to you." She put down her empty glass and stood to leave. "I'm so sorry I'm the one who had to tell you."

"I knew, but now I won't keep looking for her, thinking that maybe she got away, so thank you." Liz rose to her feet.

"I can't imagine what you've been going through, but now the police will have the victim's name," Amy Sue said.

"They have to take us seriously once they know that Jack was having an affair with the woman you saw murdered," Liz argued.

"He still has an alibi." She hesitated. "There's something else. My sister is a lawyer. She thinks Jack might have killed before. You and I are now targets." Liz paled, making her freckles stand out as she hugged herself. "I'd suggest staying away from him and being careful."

"Just the opposite of what you plan to do," Liz pointed out.

Amy Sue shrugged. "I have my reasons for trying to get justice so I can sleep at night. I know this is a lot to process. It won't take much for Jack Marshall to find you—if he hasn't already. Let me give you my cell phone number." They exchanged numbers, both promising to call if they learned anything new.

AFTER THE WOMAN left, Liz considered having another drink, but instead found herself standing at the front window. She kept thinking about Whitney and Jack Marshall. She felt spooked as she watched Amy Sue go to her vehicle. Moments after the woman drove away, a set of headlights flashed on and a large dark car moved slowly down the street, disappearing behind Amy Sue's.

Hugging herself, Liz tried to shake off the feeling that the driver was following the young blonde. She let the curtain fall back in place and checked to make sure her front door was locked. Tomorrow she would have the locks changed so no one could get back in—including Robert.

She pulled out her phone to call Amy Sue and warn her when her cell rang. Robert. She hesitated. He was probably calling to check on her.

"Hey," he said when she answered. "You all right? That was pretty creepy that woman showing up like that. So you think she was telling the truth and Jack Marshall killed Whitney?"

Liz could hear bar sounds in the background. "I'm fine, thanks." She was going to have to get used to being on her own, she thought, wishing she hadn't picked up his call.

"I was thinking this could work to our advantage."

"My friend being dead?" She closed her eyes, feeling one of her headaches coming on.

"Jack Marshall. Baby, we're sitting in the catbird's seat."

"I don't know what that means, and I don't care."

"Listen, this man owes us. Owes you, Liz."

"I have no idea what you're talking about. I just found out that my best friend was murdered. I'm tired, Robert. I'm going to get a bath and go to bed."

"We know what Jack Marshall did. Baby, he's got all that money, and I'm betting he'd do just about anything to keep his secret. All we have to do—"

"*Blackmail?* Have you lost your mind? Robert, I don't want to hear this. Good night, and don't call me back when you're even drunker. I'm shutting off my phone." She disconnected, thinking it was so like her husband to try to make money out of this tragedy. As it was, he'd never really liked Whitney to start with. Turning off her phone, she made herself another drink and took it into the bathroom.

As the tub filled, she thought about her friend. That she and Whitney had even met had been a fluke. Or fate. They'd ended up roommates after Liz had put up an ad on a bulletin board at college. She'd needed money and the freshman Whitney Clark had needed a place to live. From the moment they met, even with Whitney being so much younger, they'd become fast friends. Both being sisterless, they had longed for one.

Liz shut off the water in the tub, finished her drink and stripped down to climb in. She'd failed her little sister and now Whitney was gone forever and her murderer would go free unless someone stopped him.

RUSS FELT HOG-TIED. He needed Jack Marshall's phone records for the week before and after the murder. He also needed to know which private planes had flown to and from Great Falls and Billings the night of the murder. Both required a warrant, which there was no chance the chief would authorize. He also really could have used a cadaver dog before any more construction was done at the subdivision where Amy Sue had seen Jack Marshall kill that woman.

He'd already called a friend who worked at the airport. "How long would it take to fly a small personal plane to Great Falls from Billings?" he asked.

"Hour and a half."

Too much time. "How about one of these jets you say fly in and out all the time?"

"Fifty minutes. You taking a trip?" his friend asked.

"I wish." After he hung up, he knew that had to be

the way Marshall had managed it the night of the murder. Fifty minutes if the jet was waiting. He gets dropped off at the airport where he's left his car. There would be a record of him leaving it, taking it out and returning it that night. Unless he used dealer plates and cash.

Russ felt as if he were spinning his wheels. He thought he'd figured out how Marshall could have done it. But he still couldn't prove it.

Rubbing his neck, he knew contacting Marshall wasn't going to get the answers he needed. He felt stymied. But he kept trying even knowing that when the chief got wind of it, he'd be gone. At least tonight he was still a detective with the Billings Police Department. Tomorrow, he might not be.

He thought of Amy Sue. He recalled the terror in her eyes that first night. He couldn't give up.

AMY SUE SHOT a glance in her rearview mirror not for the first time tonight. Since leaving Liz Baker's house, she hadn't been able to shake off the feeling that someone was following her. It was impossible with all the traffic to tell if she was being tailed, yet the hair rose on the back of her neck as she drove. The night was dark, much like the night of the murder. It wasn't that far to the hotel, but with the traffic, it seemed to take forever.

All she could think about was getting to her room and locking herself inside. Earlier with the detective she'd felt so safe. It was her own feelings that had felt dangerous. After her first and only experience falling in love had ended so disastrously, she'd thought she'd never feel that way again.

But soft-spoken Russell with his warm brown eyes

and his smile had gotten past the walls she'd built around her heart. He'd made her realize that she could love again, although the timing couldn't have been worse.

When she'd started this, she'd known it would be dangerous. She hadn't cared. She'd felt like a shell of a person. But now, she was afraid because she didn't want to die. She wanted to live, and she didn't want to miss a minute of it.

A horn honked behind her. Her gaze shot to her rearview mirror again. The driver of a large truck honked again, and she realized the light had changed. Hurriedly, she got her SUV going, promising herself she would pay more attention to the road.

She checked her mirror again. A large black SUV was now behind her, the driver in shadow as the glare of the streetlights swept past. When she looked again, the SUV was gone. A pickup had taken its place behind her.

As she neared the hotel, she tried to relax. She couldn't let her feelings for Russ make her forget what she was doing here. The two of them were going to see that justice was done.

The parking lot was full. The only spot was some distance from the entrance. As she pulled in, a vehicle passed behind her, someone also looking for a parking spot? Turning off the engine, she sat for a moment. The night seemed darker, the tall lights illuminating the lot dim and distant.

Grabbing her purse, she opened her door and stepped out, hesitating for a moment to listen. She could hear traffic on the nearby street but little else. Her cell rang. It was her sister.

"Josie," she said as she locked the car and headed

through the parked cars toward the hotel entrance. It was such a relief to hear her sister's voice. Just the sound of it made her feel safer. "How's the trial going?"

"I'd rather talk about how you're doing."

"I got the name of the woman I saw murdered."

"Amy Sue, how in the world did you do that?"

"It's a long story, and I can't get into it right now."

"Where are you?"

"I just got to the hotel. I'm in the parking lot." Before Josie spoke, she heard footfalls behind her and turned to see a man headed in her direction. He was large and bundled up even though the night wasn't that cold. She began to walk faster as she listened to her sister warn her about parking lots.

"There's someone following me," she said into the phone. "I might have to run."

"Don't hang up. Run!"

She took off running hard toward the lights of the hotel lobby glowing in the distance. She didn't dare look behind her for fear he would soon be breathing down her neck or worse. A car pulled into the lot, the headlights blinding her, forcing her to slow and move to the side as it passed.

She looked back. There was no sign of the man. Her pulse thundered in her ears. Had he cut through the cars? She couldn't see him, but that didn't mean that he wasn't there waiting to grab her and haul her back into the nest of large SUVs in the lot.

"What's happening?" Josie demanded.

Unable to speak, she ran the rest of the way to the hotel entrance, slowing as she mounted the steps before turning to look back. At first, she didn't see him. Then he moved out of the edge of the darkness before he turned and disappeared into the parked vehicles.

"Was it Marshall?" her sister asked.

"He was wearing a hoodie and jeans and stayed in the shadows, and it was too dark to see his face, but who else?"

· "Hang up and call Detective Tate. Then call me back."

Chapter Seventeen

The next morning, the moment Russ saw Amy Sue coming out of the hotel elevator, he could see the change in her. It made him think of the near-hysterical woman who'd come to the police station to report the murder she'd witnessed. Nothing like the woman he'd taken to a fast-food lunch. The woman he saw now had been scared last night when she'd called but was now in control. It was if he'd watched her growing stronger right before his eyes.

He saw it at once. She was tired of being a victim, and now she was coming out fighting. He'd seen the look before as a street cop. That moment when an abusive woman had had enough. There was fear, too, but a defiance that was good to see. It always filled him with hope that the woman would triumph.

Seeing the look on Amy Sue's face, though, didn't give him hope. It scared the hell out of him. This woman was going up against Goliath, and he knew it wouldn't be a fair fight. She was determined before, but now she was out for blood.

But it was the way her look softened when she saw him, the smile that curled at her lips, the shine in those blue eyes that stilled his heart. She was dressed much as she had been last night in boots, jeans and a jean jacket. Her long hair was pulled back in a ponytail. This morning, she looked young and alive, and he desperately wanted to keep her that way.

Last night, he'd searched the parking lot but of course Marshall was long gone. He didn't doubt for a moment that the man had tried to scare her again. It was the escalating of the threats that worried him. Amy Sue had wanted to "rattle the man's cage"—well, she had. But now what would Marshall do? How far would he go?

They'd gone up to a lounge on her hotel room floor last night so she could tell him her news. She'd understood why he didn't want to talk at the police station. She hadn't been comfortable talking in her hotel room. Neither had he.

They'd ordered food and beverages from room service and ate while she'd told him all about the redhead she'd seen in the dealership parking lot and on impulse had followed her to Marshall's office.

That hadn't surprised him. But the conversation she'd overheard had. Clearly, she hadn't heeded his advice to stay clear of Marshall.

She had proceeded to tell him how she'd followed the woman to her house in Park City, south of Billings. "I had no idea what I was going to say when she opened the door, and then I saw a photograph of a woman on a table in her entryway and recognized her as the woman I saw murdered. Her name is Whitney Clark, and she's been missing for just over two weeks, so the timeline adds up."

"This woman you spoke with—"

"Liz Baker, soon to be Jones. Divorce."

"—she knows for certain Marshall was seeing her friend."

"She saw him leaving the house Whitney had been renting in Laurel. I have her cell number." She had pulled out her phone and given it to him.

He hadn't been able to contain his smile. "And you thought you wouldn't make a good investigator."

She had flushed at his words. "I was so good that I didn't notice the large dark car that followed me to Liz's house—and then to my hotel. I'm worried about Liz. Jack Marshall now knows where she lives."

"You definitely make one hell of a detective," he'd told her. "But I'm worried that both you and Liz Baker are now in danger. He knows where you're both staying. I suggest you move to another hotel. I'll see what I can do about getting Liz to leave her house for a while since now she's in danger—just like you."

She had agreed to move, and they finished their meals, talking until it was late. He'd carried her suitcase out to her car, and she'd followed him to another hotel in his neighborhood.

Even with all the new information, including the missing woman's name and a friend who would swear Marshall and Whitney Clark were having an affair, Russ knew it wasn't enough to open an investigation.

But he also knew he would have to take the information to the chief and let the chips fall where they may. He planned to go into the office after seeing Amy Sue this morning. He'd wanted to make sure she was all right first. He should have known she would be.

Last night before he'd left her at another hotel, they'd stood just inside the empty lobby. He had desperately wanted to take her in his arms, tell her he wouldn't let anything happen to her. Hell, what he really wanted to do was kiss her.

But it was inappropriate given that he was the detective and she was the eyewitness—even if there wasn't a case, because he had to believe that there would be a case and Marshall would go down for homicide.

As he approached her this morning, he felt almost shy. Their first encounter at the police station hadn't gone well, but their lunch together had gone better, he thought. She'd made it clear even at the fast-food place that she didn't trust him, yet she'd called him on his cell rather than 911 when she was in trouble last night. That gave him hope. They'd gotten close last night, but could he hope that she might share any of his feelings when this was over? She seemed wary, as if she'd been betrayed before. They had that in common, he thought. They were both leery, as they should be when it came to falling in love. But this, whatever it was sparking between them, felt like a fresh beginning for them both.

As he reached her, she looked up, her smile broadening, giving him hope. He noticed the way her blue eyes changed colors. At the police station they'd been more gray, but here in this light, they were a clear, Montana-summer-sky blue.

He glanced around the hotel lobby, then at her. "Wanna go somewhere?" To his surprise, she nodded. "There's a café not far from here where we can have some privacy and maybe even breakfast if you're hungry."

She chuckled. "Are you really worried about keeping me fed, or is it just an excuse to spend time with me?"

He grinned, shaking his head. "I must be so transparent," he said as he led her out the door. They walked the few blocks to the café through the crisp early June morning. The mountains in the distance were still snow-capped. Summer was still probably another snowstorm away.

The café was hardly ever busy with mostly locals who lived close by in the blue-collar neighborhood. The gray-haired waitress said, "Mornin', Russ. Whatcha need?" He glanced at Amy Sue, who seemed amused that everyone they'd come across in the café seemed to know him.

"Coffee. Black," she said.

"Two coffees and two of your pineapple Danish." He glanced guiltily at Amy Sue. "My weakness," he said as he led her through the café to a private room at the back.

They took a seat and waited for their coffees and the Danishes. The waitress showed up only moments later with a cup of coffee in each hand, the plate of Danish balancing on her wrist. She smoothly deposited all of it with a cheerful, "Enjoy!" and left, closing the door after her.

"You come here often?" Amy Sue joked.

"I spent time here with my grandparents on my mother's side. Been coming here for years. My grandfather was the cook, my grandmother the baker. You should try the Danish. It's her recipe." He saw her surprise. He also saw her relax a little. What time they'd been thrown together they'd talked about the murder, Marshall, evidence, their frustration. He liked seeing her relax here.

They talked about their childhoods, his on the ranch and here in this café, hers on the family ranch and farm outside of Dry Gulch. There was so much he wanted to say to her, he just hoped they had the time for him to do it.

It surprised Amy Sue and worried her a little as to how much she was enjoying being here with this cowboy detective. So it was no wonder that when the conversation turned personal, she steered it back. "My sister thinks Jack Marshall might have killed before."

He nodded. "I don't believe it was the first time he's done something like this."

She stared at him astonished. *"So he has killed before?"*

"I found evidence that in high school, he was questioned by the police about a former girlfriend who was attacked and hospitalized for her injuries. Like this time, he had an alibi. His new girlfriend swore they'd been together all night. His attacked ex-girlfriend accused him at first, but later retracted it, saying she didn't get a good look at her assailant. It would appear that he got away with it."

"Just like he's trying to do now."

"I haven't quit investigating from the moment you walked through that door saying you'd just witnessed a murder, but I might not be a homicide detective long enough to see this through. I'm getting a lot of pressure from the higher-ups to stop."

"You could lose your job?"

"I'm more worried about letting you down or failing to keep you from getting killed."

Amy Sue sat back and took a breath. "I'm just afraid that no matter what I do, Jack Marshall is going to get away with murder. I suspect you are worried about that, too, Detective."

He laughed. "Isn't it time you called me Russ?"

"Russ." She liked the sound of it on her lips and felt

heat rush to her center as their gazes met. His eyes were a rich warm brown like melted dark chocolate, his lashes long. It struck her how handsome he was, especially when he smiled.

But it was the look in those eyes that sent butterflies flitting around in her chest. Like a lightning bolt, she felt the electricity of it spiking not just desire, but an aching need she'd never felt so strongly before. Russ's look promised so much more than she'd ever dreamed possible.

Amy Sue swallowed and glanced away to reach for her fork and cut off a piece of the pineapple Danish. She could feel her fear of letting a man into her heart again. As she put the bite in her mouth and chewed, she felt shaken by the look that had passed between them. She instantly doubted it, telling herself that he was only being nice. Only doing his job.

But when she looked up again, she knew something real was happening between them. It had never felt more real. Russ was taking a chance on her, one that could cost him his career. Not just that, she realized. She'd seen both desire and that aching need in him as well. They both wanted this, needed it.

"What do you think?" he asked and smiled. For a moment, she felt confused and didn't have any idea what he meant. "The Danish. Have you ever tasted anything like it?"

She licked her lips and laughed. "I haven't. It's amazing. Do you mind if I..." She nodded toward the rest of the one she'd taken a bite from.

"It's all yours," Russ said, sounding pleased. He had wanted her to like his grandmother's concoction as well as the café. Mostly, though, he wanted her to like him and she did. "I'm really glad you like it."

Nodding, she more than liked this man. Her instincts told her that she could trust him not just with her life but with her heart. She wasn't sure if she was the one who leaned in for the kiss or if Russ had initiated it. Not that it mattered.

The moment his lips touched hers, she felt the ground under her feel solid for the first time in months. He cupped the back of her neck, drawing her closer as he deepened the kiss. She knew that she would never taste pineapple again and not remember this moment and the joy of their first kiss.

Even as they drew apart, she could tell it wouldn't be their last. There was something as solid as the ground in Russ's look, a staying power that said he.was in this for the long haul.

Now if they could just stay alive, she thought as her cell phone rang.

Chapter Eighteen

Amy Sue didn't return her sister's call until after Russ walked her back to the hotel.

"I'm worried about you," Josie said without preamble when she answered. It was the lawyer in her, Amy Sue told herself. Or maybe the second sight she had on occasion. Josie *hadn't* been worried about her going to Billings alone for a week and look how that had turned out. But if she'd seen anything bad happening beforehand, she hadn't said anything.

"Has your second sight come back?" she asked between bites of cold fries. She was joking, kind of. When Josie didn't answer right away, she was alarmed and said, "It has, hasn't it?"

"Maybe, a little. I don't know for sure," her sister said. "Of course, I'm worried about you given the kind of man Jack Marshall is. I have a really bad feeling."

Amy Sue had known that anything she did to get justice for the murdered woman was putting her in danger. But her sister telling her about her so-called bad feeling felt more real and terrifying than she wanted to admit. Like their grandmother, Josie had seen things before they happened. She said she sensed them, a darkness she saw coming.

When Amy Sue came to Billings to prove Jack Marshall was a killer, she'd been angry because she hadn't been believed. But she'd also wanted justice, and not just for what Marshall had done. She wanted justice for what had happened to her last year. A man had tried to kill her, but the real pain was that he'd made her trust him only to break her heart. Getting justice for that then-unknown woman Marshall had tricked and murdered had made her fearless.

She no longer felt fearless. Detective Russell Tate had made her want to believe in love again and a future she could only dream possible. The only thing she was willing to risk now was her heart with him. But she'd made a promise not just to herself but to Liz and even Whitney. She couldn't go back on that any more than Russ could stop trying to get justice as part of this job—even if he lost that job.

Last night after Russ had arrived so quickly following her call, she had let her sister know that she was safe and that the detective was with her.

Now she filled Josie in on what she'd discovered yesterday. "The dead woman's name is Whitney Clark. Russ is following up on it, but we still need to find someone to verify our suspicions as to how Jack Marshall pulled it off given his alibi."

"We?" Josie asked.

Amy Sue heard the caution in her sister's voice all in that one word. "I'm not getting in over my head with Russ if that's what you're worried about." Even as she said the words, she thought of the look she'd seen in his eyes and recalled her own reaction to it—and the kiss.

"Russ? Oh Amy Sue."

"You need to stop worrying about me."

"I wish I could, but you're my sister and I love you and you're in Billings rattling the cage, as you put it, of a murderer and now I have this bad feeling."

"When you put it that way," she joked. "Actually, I've run out of ideas. I've done as much as I can, and so has Russ." What she didn't say was what she was thinking. Whatever happened next was in Jack Marshall's court, and truthfully, that did have her worried. Not just for herself. The last time she talked to Liz Baker she'd gotten the impression the woman might do something desperate.

"Russ plans to call Marshall in to the police department after he talks to Liz, so I guess we'll see what happens. How is your trial going?"

"Fine. Call me when you hear something and, in the meantime, please stay away from Jack Marshall and be really careful."

Amy Sue smiled ruefully as she disconnected, having heard what her sister hadn't needed to say. *Be careful with that cowboy detective, too.*

LIZ TURNED HER phone back on first thing that morning to see that she had three calls from her ex. She was about to delete them without listening to her ex-husband's drunken ramblings when Detective Tate called.

"Can we meet and talk?" he asked after introducing himself and telling her he'd talked to Amy Sue Brand. They agreed to meet at the bar where Liz worked in Laurel rather than her making the drive into Billings to the police department.

"I have the early shift today, but it shouldn't be busy. We can talk there, if that's all right," she told him.

After she disconnected, she remembered what her ex had said the night before about blackmailing Jack Marshall. She thought it was all talk, but it was just like him to get into trouble. Against her better judgment, she listened to his first voicemail.

I'm going to do this thing I told you about because I want you back, Liz, and I don't want to fight about money anymore. Imagine what we could do with a whole lot of money. Just think about it.

She shook her head and listened to the next one. Robert sounded a lot less sober. *I'll do anything to get you back. Anything. I just wanted you to know how much I love you.*

Liz almost didn't listen to the last voicemail, expecting it would just be more of the same. She'd heard it all before, how much her ex loved her, but this time she wasn't going back to him no matter what he did. If he actually did what he was suggesting, blackmailing Jack Marshall, he'd be going to prison.

Liz. Something in Robert's voice scared her. *I did it. There's no going back now. I set up a meeting tonight. Once I get the money—* The rest of the voicemail was lost in the sound of the bar noise.

"Oh, Robert, what have you done?" She deleted the voicemails thinking she was protecting her ex. She owed him at least that much, she thought as she left for work.

Liz Baker was right. The place was empty when Russ arrived to find her stocking beer behind the bar. "You must be Detective Tate," she said, wiping her hands on a towel before coming around the bar to motion to a seat at one of the tables.

Russ found himself assessing the woman as she told him about her friend Whitney, how she hadn't heard from her for over two weeks, not since the night her friend's lover was taking her to their new house that was under construction.

"That was the last time I heard from her," Liz said. "I expected her to call either that night late or the next day. She didn't call, and I started getting worried. I knew she'd be excited about the house and want to tell me everything."

"Amy Sue Brand said she recognized a photo you had of Whitney on a table in your entry." She nodded. "You have other photos of your friend?"

Liz pulled out her phone, called up something and handed him the cell.

"Mind if I send these to my phone?" She didn't. He handed her cell back and listened as she told him about her visit to the car dealer.

"He lied right to my face, but it was him. What gave him away was when he first saw me, he was startled because he recognized me, I know he did. Whitney had a photo of the two of us at her house."

"But before then, he didn't know who you were?"

She nodded. "But he does now." She shuddered and looked toward the bar's front door. "I saw a car follow Amy Sue last night. I was worried it was him."

"Someone did follow her to her hotel. She's since changed hotels. You might consider staying with someone for a while."

Liz shook her head. "He's not going to put me out of my house."

He wanted to argue the point, but saved his breath. "Do you own a firearm?"

"Of course. I'm a Montanan born and bred." She narrowed her eyes. "You seem to think I'm going to need it."

"Would you pull the trigger if Jack Marshall broke into your house?" he asked.

"In less than a heartbeat."

Russ thanked her and rose. "I'm going to take this information to the chief, but if I were you, I wouldn't expect much to happen."

"Marshall's alibi, right? Amy Sue told me. There has to be some way to discredit it, right?"

"I'm working on it. But in the meantime, I would suggest you never leave work without someone following you out to your car to make sure you're safe. You might also want to reconsider staying with a friend for a while and not going back to your house."

"Thanks for the advice, but I can take care of myself."

A couple of what looked like regulars came into the bar arguing about fossil fuel versus those damned electric cars as Russ left, but not before he gave Liz his cell phone number. He hoped he didn't have to tell her again to be careful of the man who'd murdered her friend.

Chapter Nineteen

Russ wanted to go straight to the chief with what he had, but he knew it wasn't enough to get a real investigation going. He would also be jeopardizing his job even further. Better to wait until he had something solid.

He did, however, share what he'd learned with his partner, and wasn't surprised at Hanson's reaction.

"What the hell are you doing?" Hanson demanded. "You were told to back off Marshall. I can't believe you're still chasing this."

"I have a missing woman, the same woman Amy Sue saw murdered, and a witness who says the woman's lover was Jack Marshall. Is that really not enough to make you wonder how the bastard did it?"

His partner shook his head. "You have a missing woman, period. Adding some third party willing to say Jack Marshall was the woman's lover doesn't prove anything except the man is a philanderer. You still don't have any proof that the woman is even dead, let alone murdered by her lover—who we all know was in Great Falls at a conference."

"Except he was also looking to buy a private jet, which would have gotten him to and from Billings that night in enough time to kill his mistress and still get back to Great Falls before anyone realized he was missing."

"Have you found someone who flew him? I didn't think so," Hanson said.

"What about the eyewitness who saw Marshall murder Whitney Clark?" Russ demanded. "The man is lying. And it isn't the first time he got someone to lie for him. Years go his ex-girlfriend was attacked. Marshall's new girlfriend gave him an alibi—and he got away with it. How many more women has he hurt or killed?"

"Are you listening to yourself?" Hanson demanded. "You make it sound as if Jack Marshall is a serial killer!"

"Why not? I'm sure he's a serial cheater."

His partner shook his head. "You really need to let this go. If the chief knew how much time you're putting into this—let alone that you're digging into Marshall's past—"

"I've been doing it on my own time," Tate said.

"Like that would make a difference." His partner swore. "Unless you have a body and can put Marshall in Billings that night, you're wasting your time. Not to mention, if the chief finds out, I'm going to be looking for a new partner. Is this woman really worth losing your job over?"

"It's not about a woman. It's about justice, something Whitney Clark can't seem to get in Billings, Montana, because of the man she fell in love with—Jack Marshall— and the people who protect him—even the police."

He sat down and lwrote up his report. He wanted this on the record. Eventually the truth would come out, he told himself. He wanted to be on the right side of the law when it did.

Russ had just finished when the report came in about a body being found in a pickup on the rims last night. The victim was Robert Baker.

Liz got the call from Detective Tate later than afternoon. The moment he said, "I have some bad news," she feared it was going to be about Amy Sue.

"Your ex-husband Robert was found murdered on the rimrocks overlooking the city in the wee hours of the morning. I'm so sorry."

She'd dropped into a chair as she fought conflicting emotions. There was the usual sorrow and regret when it came to Robert, but also an old ache for the man she'd thought she'd married. The news, while sad and tragic, didn't come as a shock. "I knew this was going to happen. I tried to stop him." She spilled the whole blackmail story to the detective.

"Do you still have those voicemails he left you?" Tate asked.

"No, I foolishly deleted them to protect him. Won't they be on his phone?"

"His phone is missing," the detective said.

"You know who did this," she said, anger making her eyes burn with fresh tears. "Jack Marshall killed him."

"We might suspect that was the case, but we have no proof."

"How was he killed?"

"He was stabbed to death and the scene made to look like a robbery."

Liz let out a bitter laugh. "Like Robert appeared to be a man with a lot of money driving that beat-up old truck, dressing the way he did?"

"I understand what you're saying," Tate said. "The murder will continue to be under investigation. I will need a statement from you to take to the chief, but Liz, if you're right, Marshall will have an alibi. You can count on that."

"YOU MUST HAVE gotten in late," Christine said to her husband that morning at breakfast.

"Not all that late. Ten thirty. You were already asleep," Jack said, not meeting her gaze. "I didn't want to wake you. I had a lot on my mind, so I slept in the guest room."

She'd heard him come home after 3:00 a.m. She had immediately realized that he'd been drinking. It was the way he'd taken the stairs. She'd turned over, away from his side of the bed, and pretended to be asleep as she'd tried not to be alarmed by how late he'd come dragging in. Whatever was going on with her husband was bad, that much she knew. He'd left their bedroom, stumbling down the hallway to the guest room.

"Is it something you'd like to talk about?" she offered as she poured him a cup of coffee and one for herself.

"Just business. It's nothing to worry about. Thanks," he said as he took the coffee and offered her a smile.

"I wish you had woken me last night. I've missed you." She returned his smile and touched his hand. They had sex regularly, she made sure of that. But she realized it had been over two weeks and during that time, she'd hardly seen him because of the late hours he'd been keeping. She worried that the affair hadn't ended or had ended badly, and he was still dealing with it. Yet she couldn't ask, could she? It was the hole she'd dug for herself. Sometimes she questioned if Jack was even aware that she knew more about him than he even seemed to know about himself. She found it almost amusing that he thought he was keeping his affairs from her.

"I'm sorry," he said, turning his hand to take hers. "I did think about waking you, but you looked like you were sleeping so good, I couldn't do it."

She wondered if her smile was convincing as she listened to his lie. "I wish you would have. Maybe come home earlier tonight?"

He nodded and let go of her hand. "Make us a reservation to your favorite restaurant. We'll make a night of it."

Christine had barely agreed when she heard the doorbell chime. When she looked out and saw the police car parked out front, she felt her heart drop. She glanced at her husband and glimpsed something she'd never seen in his eyes.

Panic.

Chapter Twenty

"Detective Russell Tate," the police officer said by way of introduction when she opened the door. "Is your husband at home?"

"Yes," Christine said as she stepped aside to let him enter. "Please come in. Jack and I were just finishing up breakfast." As she led the way, she asked over her shoulder, "Can I get you a cup of coffee?"

"No, thank you. I just need to speak with your husband."

She saw that Jack was still sitting at the breakfast bar, holding a mug of coffee in both hands probably to keep them from shaking, she thought. "What's this about, Detective?"

"It would probably be best if I spoke to your husband alone, Mrs. Marshall," the detective said.

Christine looked to Jack. Their gazes met but only for an instant as he quickly looked away. She noticed, too, that he hadn't asked the detective what this was about. She feared he already knew. "I'll be upstairs if you need me."

"Before you go," the detective said, "can you tell me what time your husband came home last night?"

She pretended surprise. "It was a little after ten. He'd worked late."

"He was home the rest of the night?"

"Of course," she said frowning. "We're remodeling, and I wanted him to see some of the ideas the designers have come up with that we needed to act on by today." She noticed that the detective wasn't looking at her, but at Jack.

"Is that right, Mr. Marshall?" There was an edge to the cop's voice that she couldn't ignore. Detective Tate knew it was a lie and probably not the first one her husband had told him.

Jack cleared his voice. He didn't look at her even though she hadn't lied, she'd merely repeated what he'd told her. "That's right."

"What's happened?" she asked, since it was clear her husband wasn't going to for obvious reasons.

"There was a murder last night." The detective was looking at her again now. "Do you know a man by the name of Robert Baker?" She thought for a moment before she shook her head. "He was killed in the early morning after leaving a downtown bar. Stabbed and robbed."

Her shocked expression was real. Stabbed and robbed? "Why would you think my husband would know anything about that?" she demanded.

"Because I have reason to believe your husband was being blackmailed by the victim."

Jack was on his feet so quickly that he knocked over the breakfast bar stool. "Detective, my wife has told you that I was home last night when this man was murdered. I don't want to have to call the chief of police to get this cleared up, but I know nothing about blackmail or this man who was killed."

Christine knew that her husband's angry denial was more for her than the detective. Yet she was stunned. For a moment she thought the detective might arrest her husband. He certainly looked as if he wanted to badly enough.

But he didn't move. He stood waiting, for what, she didn't know. Then he turned to her, "Sorry to have bothered you." He tipped his Western hat and saw his way out.

After he left, Jack moved slowly over to the downed stool and picked it up. "That detective has it out for me."

She wanted to ask why the cop thought Jack was being blackmailed—and for what, but she weighed her options and opted not to ask. Stabbed and robbed? Obviously, the detective had it wrong. Jack was guilty of something, but he couldn't be involved in a murder. She thought about last night, hearing the guest room shower running past three in the morning. It had to be a woman who'd kept her husband out so late.

It is best not to know, her mother had told her. *People like us live separate lives in a marriage. The husband takes care of his business, the wife takes care of hers and keeps the family together. If you ask, he might tell you, and you don't want that especially if the law ever gets involved.*

She shuddered to think what kind of marriage her mother had endured and told herself she wouldn't allow that to happen to her own no matter what she had to do.

AMY SUE WAS shocked when she recived Liz's phone call about Robert. "I'm so sorry." Liz told her about the voice-mails she'd received from her ex the night before.

Amy Sue couldn't believe it. "He was planning to blackmail Jack Marshall?"

"The last time I heard from him, he said he'd already sent the blackmail demand and was going to meet up with him. You know Marshall killed him."

"Oh, Liz, I'm sorry."

"Sorry Robert was such a loser? I know I shouldn't speak ill of the dead, but I knew the kind of man he was. It's why I divorced him. He was always out for a fast buck. I know I must sound heartless, but he was never going to change. He lost all of our savings time and time again on get-rich-quick schemes that turned into scams. He just never learned. I tried to stop him last night, but…"

"Is Detective Tate investigating the murder?" Amy Sue asked.

"He said it looked like a robbery that went wrong, but I don't believe it." Amy Sue didn't either. "You know Marshall will have an alibi."

"I'm just worried about you," she said. If Marshall killed Robert like they suspected, then it felt as if he was out of control and even more dangerous.

"I'm going to the police station this morning to file a missing person's report on Whitney," Liz said. "Detective Tate says that's all we can do for now. He said it might be possible to get the voicemails from Robert off my phone, but that it wouldn't prove that Jack Marshall killed Robert."

After warning Liz to be careful, she called Russ's cell number. "Is it true? Do you think Jack Marshall killed Liz's ex?"

"I know it looks like that might have been the case given what we know about the blackmail," he said. "But Robert had been drinking heavily at the bar. He'd won quite a lot at the pool table and was flashing it around as he left and bragging about how he was going to be rich. It's possible someone at the bar followed him planning to rob him and things got violent."

"It's just such a coincidence, isn't it, if someone else killed him," she said. "Are you going to bring Marshall in for questioning?"

"I already talked to him. His wife gave him an alibi for last night. If I push it any further it could be the last straw with my boss. It might already be too late if Marshall calls the chief about this. All I can do is lay out what I have to the chief, but I don't think it is going to be enough to convince him to open an investigation against the man even if we had the voicemails Robert sent Liz. All the evidence is circumstantial."

"Except that now you think the wife has lied for him."

"Only if he wasn't with her last night," Russ pointed out.

"I had thought about paying her a visit. She should know what's been going on. I really doubt her husband has told her."

"She might already know. She could be part of it," he said. "Things are often not what they seem. I'd steer clear of her if I were you."

Amy Sue knew the wife might know or at least suspect, but she couldn't imagine her being involved other than keeping quiet. "I've met her. She had a fit over breaking a nail at the salon. I can't see her lugging her husband's dead lover from a house to the trunk of his car out of the goodness of her heart."

"No one knows what goes on in a marriage," he said, sounding as if he had firsthand knowledge. They'd never talked about their personal lives, at least not about former relationships. Had he been married? Was he still married? The thought surprised her. He might have a wife back at the ranch. She recalled looking at his left hand. No wedding band. But that didn't mean anything. A lot of ranchers didn't wear a ring because it was dangerous working around equipment.

She thought of those hands of his, his long fingers, the nails clipped short. There was something reassuring about them, but also sensual. She shivered at the thought of those hands on her body, and felt an ache of longing to find out.

"What now?" she asked, dragging her thoughts back to why she was in Billings and not on the farm where she belonged.

"I have to take what I have to the chief."

She heard the worry in his voice. "He won't fire you, will he?"

"Maybe he'll surprise me and open an investigation against Jack Marshall."

AFTER THE DETECTIVE LEFT, Christine couldn't look at her husband. She'd lied for him. It was the first time he'd put her in this position. She told herself it would be the last. No matter what her mother had put up with, Christine wasn't going to do this. It was humiliating. She couldn't let him drag her name and reputation through the mud. She had let him "have his cake and eat it, too," as her mother called it, but something had happened this time that changed everything.

"Christine, I—"

Her cell rang, and she hurriedly reached for her phone, snatching it up and leaving the room to take the call. It was a fellow board member on the charitable foundation they both had seats on. Misty wanted to talk, and Christine let her, half listening to the woman go on about one of the other board members, while also listening for Jack to leave for work. She kept thinking of the look on his face when the detective had arrived.

By the time she got off the call, Jack had left just as she'd hoped. She felt relieved and yet afraid that he'd want to confess all of his sins and clear his conscience. She'd never wanted to hear about any of the women he'd had affairs with, let alone whatever he'd done recently that had a homicide detective at their door first thing in the morning.

She needed time to think, but right now she had to get ready for her nail appointment and after that, she had a lunch date. She couldn't cancel. She needed to pretend that everything was fine—just as Jack had been doing when she'd known he was in trouble.

Later, she would decide what to do about her husband.

Jack had never been much of a drinker, but right now he would have loved to go to a bar and drink himself half blind. His head ached from lack of sleep and fear, and he was a little hung over from last night. Nothing had gone as planned, and for a man who usually planned each move painstakingly, he found himself off-kilter and running scared.

After leaving the house to avoid Christine, the first thing he'd done once he was in his vehicle was call the chief of police. The moment Milt answered, he told him how Detective Tate had come to his house first thing this morning to accuse him of murdering yet another person. "He has it out for me, that's all I can think."

"I'll take care of it," Milt promised, but he didn't sound as upset as Jack had thought he should have been. "Was this the body that was discovered up on the rims?"

"How should I know?" Jack demanded. "I had no idea what the man was talking about."

"Okay, okay. Let me handle it."

Their conversation had ended abruptly, leaving him uneasy.

After he'd disconnected, all he could think about was Christine. She hadn't been able to look at him after the detective left, but she'd covered for him. Even if she knew that he'd lied about coming home around ten thirty last night, she wouldn't believe that he'd kill some man up on the rims. He couldn't imagine that she'd even believe that her husband was being blackmailed.

He realized that he was more worried about what Christine believed than the chief of police. Milt would go along with whatever he said, always had, nothing would be different this time, right?

Except this time there was a body. He rubbed a hand over his face as he pulled into his parking spot at the dealership. He'd really messed up. Last night he'd lost his temper. The moment he met Robert Baker he knew this bum would bleed him dry. The thought had made him furious. He'd been glad that he'd thought to bring a knife for protection. He told himself that he hadn't planned to kill him, but wondered if it was true. Lately, he'd been so damned angry.

Now he was about to get out of the car when he saw Whitney's good friend Liz heading toward him across the parking lot.

Chapter Twenty-One

Liz had never been more nervous in her life. She'd been waiting in the parking lot for Jack Marshall. She'd been beginning to think he'd taken the day off after killing her ex-husband.

She was almost surprised when he showed up. Clearly killing must not bother him as much as what she was about to do. She'd called work and had no trouble getting the day off once they knew about Robert being murdered the night before.

But there was no way she was planning to hang around the house. She had too much on her mind. A part of her wanted to get the pistol Robert had bought her when they'd separated and go pay Jack Marshall a visit he would never forget.

The thought of prison for killing the son of a B wasn't worth it, she soon realized. No, the real pay she wanted for the deaths of Whitney and Robert was that smug Jack Marshall behind bars. Unfortunately, it looked like he would keep slipping the knot on the noose.

Now as she crossed the parking lot, moving quickly toward his vehicle, she clutched the pistol in her jacket pocket and promised herself she wouldn't shoot him. Not unless she had to, she amended.

He put down the driver's-side window as she approached. From his expression, he wasn't too worried. She was on his turf, and while none of his salesmen seemed to be around, there could be someone watching from the large glass windows at the front of the showroom.

"Let's go for a test drive," Liz said as she walked around the front of the car with the dealer plates. She heard him unlock the passenger side. Grabbing the handle, she opened the door and slid into the deep plush seat. "Nice car."

He looked over at her, and she swore that if he asked her what this was about, she would shoot him. Fortunately, he started the car and pulled out of the lot. "Any place in particular?"

"Drive to your bank." He swiveled his head in her direction, his expression surprised, but he didn't say anything. "You're going to make a withdrawal." She saw his jaw tense, his lips forming a straight line across his handsome face. "I've been trying to decide how much my ex-husband's life was worth. You're lucky, it wasn't worth all that much. How much did he try to blackmail you for?" When he didn't answer, she said, "Doesn't matter. Tell you what. Make it fifty thousand."

"I can't get that much out without raising suspicion."

"Oh, please. You're such a smooth talker, and fifty grand is nothing for you. That wouldn't even buy one of the cheaper cars on your lot. I'm sure you can convince your banker to give you the money. By the way, I know where you bank. I'll wait in the car—on the phone with your wife." He tensed but kept driving.

"She always wanted a house, you know," she said. He

looked confused, as if he didn't know who she was talking about. "Whitney. She was really excited about you buying her a house."

"How do I know you won't be back next week for more money?" he asked as he pulled into the parking lot at the bank.

"You don't, but I'm not greedy like Robert. He would have bled you dry. I'm sure that's why you killed him." When Jack said nothing, she realized that he must have thought she was recording this for the police. "I'm not recording you. I just want the money before you go to jail."

Liz saw the way he was gripping the wheel and chuckled. "I don't think you can afford to kill me or anyone else right now. Eventually your friends at the police department aren't going to be able to protect you if one more person goes missing or ends up dead."

He parked and started to get out. "Don't take too long," she warned. "I wouldn't want to run out of things to say to your wife, Christine."

WHEN RUSS WALKED into the department, the chief stepped out of his office and motioned for him. He'd known this was coming. Marshall probably picked up his phone and called the chief the moment Russ left his house. His only hope was that Milt would listen to the evidence he'd found.

"Sounds like you've stepped in it now," his partner said as he passed his desk. "You are one hardheaded SOB, you know that, Tate?"

"I am when it comes to getting justice," he said as he kept walking.

"I'd say you're about to get more than you bargained for," Hanson said.

"Don't bother to sit down," the chief said as Russ walked through the open office door. "You won't be staying that long." Milt wagged his head as if confused by the detective. "Jack Marshall is threatening to file a harassment suit against the department because of you. He said you came to his house this morning and accused him of killing some man on the rims last night. Have you lost your mind?"

"No, sir. The man who was killed last night was blackmailing Marshall. Robert Baker had found out that Marshall had been having an affair with a woman named Whitney Clark. Clark is missing and has been since the night of the murder at the construction site. Our eyewitness has identified Clark as the woman she saw that night with Marshall."

The chief leaned back as if trying to distance himself from what Russ was saying. "Missing? So no proof the woman is even dead, right?"

"Except an eyewitness saw her killed by Marshall," Russ said.

"How is it that the eyewitness now can identify this Clark woman as the one she allegedly saw murdered?" Milt demanded.

"She's been doing some investigating on her own."

The chief shook his head. "Clearly she is out to get Jack Marshall."

"I believe she's merely determined to get some justice for the dead woman. If you open an investigation, I can get the proof needed for an arrest. But I need warrants for how Marshall flew back and forth from Great

Falls that night. I suspect he buried the body at the construction site. It might be too late to get a cadaver dog in there but—"

"Stop right there." Milt's eyes narrowed as he leaned forward. "It's bad enough that this alleged eyewitness is obsessed with seeing Jack Marshall behind bars, but now you're just as bad. Do you really believe that Jack Marshall killed some man up on the rims last night?"

"I do," Russ said. "Just as I believe he killed Whitney Clark, the woman he was having an affair with. No one is above the law, not even Jack Marshall. If he didn't do it, then open the investigation and let me prove that he didn't. Unless you're afraid of the truth."

The chief was shaking his head. "You're talking about Jack Marshall, one of the most powerful businessmen in the state, hell, the Northwest. He and Christine raise money every year to help this city, this county, this department."

"The man isn't who you want to believe he is. Imagine what that's going to do to the department when it comes out. You can't protect him anymore," Russ said as he stepped forward to lean on the desk toward the chief. "And it's going to come out. Your good friend Jack is a murderer. Imagine what will happen to you when it comes out that you repeatedly tried to stop me from investigating him. Here, I want you to have this." He tossed the paperwork on the man's desk.

"What's this?" the chief demanded picking it up. "Your resignation?"

"No, it's a copy of my sworn affidavit outlining the evidence I found against Jack Marshall following the eyewitness showing up at the police station after seeing him murder a woman," Russ said. "It's all there, including Liz Baker's ex-husband's attempt to blackmail Marshall and his untimely death later that night."

Breathing hard, Milt took the papers into his two fists and tore them in half and then again into fourths before pitching them into the trash beside his desk.

"That won't make the evidence go away," Russ said. "My fear is that he's going to kill again."

The chief was shaking his head. "Jack Marshall?" he said as if it was inconceivable. He looked as if he might explode. "I warned you. You have disregarded my orders for the last time. You're suspended. It's time for you to go back to the ranch. You don't belong here."

Russ nodded. "I'd tell you that you're making a mistake, but you're right," he said as he removed his gun and badge and laid them on the chief's desk. "I don't belong in a department where a man like Jack Marshall gets away with murder. But then neither do you."

With that, Russ straightened and walked out. Behind him, he heard Milt wipe everything off his desk onto the floor. He heard a loud crash, then swearing.

Hanson gave him a questioning look as he walked to his desk. "Should I start looking for a new partner?"

"Sure, why not. I'm suspended, but I'm sure he'll fire me soon."

"Picked a great day for it. The chief just dumped another murder on my desk. A man was stabbed to death up on the rimrocks."

"I already told him who did it," Russ said. "Marshall's girlfriend Whitney Clark was also stabbed. Seems to be a pattern."

"Too bad we don't have her body so we could compare stab wounds," Hanson said facetiously. "Guess I'll start looking for a new partner since it sounds like your days here are numbered."

"I wouldn't bother if I were you. Once it comes out that this department tried to keep me from investigating the murders Jack Marshall committed, you and the chief might both be looking for new jobs," Russ said. At least he could only hope. But unfortunately, he no longer had much faith in the system, he thought as he headed for the door. He thought of Amy Sue and Liz and everyone else he was letting down if he quit trying to find the truth.

But he also reminded himself that he was suspended. No service weapon and no authority to carry a gun. No badge. No right to investigate anyone. He didn't doubt for a moment that he could end up in jail if he didn't stop.

Maybe Milt was right. Maybe it was time to go back to the ranch.

JACK SHOULD HAVE known that he wasn't finished with Whitney's good friend. It was bad enough that he had to contend with Liz's ex-husband. As he walked into the bank, he tried to calm down. Fifty grand was a small price to pay for her to go away. Unlike her ex, he believed she wouldn't be back for more.

He walked to the bank manager's office door and tapped. Harold Wright looked up, smiled and waved him in. The entire transaction didn't take long, and he was walking out of the bank with the money in his briefcase. He'd have to make Harold one devil of a deal the next time he came in for a new car, but he hadn't minded.

If there was a way to put all of this behind him, Jack would have given the woman five times this much.

When he reached the car, he saw that Liz was on the phone. With Christine? He doubted that, but wouldn't put anything past her. Liz disconnected as he climbed in, taking his briefcase from him as she asked, "Any problems?"

He shook his head. He didn't think she was recording them, but he wasn't taking any chances. He'd done enough of that last night. "You can see for yourself," he said, nodding toward the briefcase.

She flipped the lock and opened it to find the large bills bound together in stacks. It took only a moment to see that the money was all there. She took it out and shoved it into her large purse. "Thanks. You should probably get to work. Christine might be on her way over there." He shot her a look. "I didn't tell her anything, if that's what you're worried about. We talked about her charity work for an interview I'm working on."

He told himself that Christine was too smart to fall for this woman wanting to interview her. Was that why his wife was headed to the dealership—if she was? Jack thought of how they'd left things this morning and grew more anxious. He could keep the fifty grand from her because he had a separate account he used for the business.

But Christine couldn't see him with this redhead.

"I'll drop you at your car," he said. "I hope this ends our business."

"It does," Liz said, sounding tired as she leaned back and closed her eyes. He saw that she had her purse on her lap, both hands on top of it. He wondered if she planned to use the money to bury her ex. Or if she had another plan for it. The money wouldn't go far. He wondered why she hadn't asked for more.

He really hoped she didn't come back for more as he

pulled into the lot and drove up next to her car. "We're here."

Liz opened her eyes, clutched her purse to her and got out. Without a word, she slammed his car door and walked over to her vehicle.

He quickly drove to his parking spot. He didn't see Christine's car. As he got out and headed for his office, he wondered if he'd made a huge mistake by paying Liz off. He'd certainly made one by killing her best friend and now her ex-husband.

She was right about one thing. He couldn't lose his temper and do anything rash again.

At least not for a while.

Chapter Twenty-Two

Amy Sue heard something in Russ's voice when he called. "What's happened?" She braced herself for the worst.

"I talked to the chief this morning, told him everything we'd learned. He doesn't think it's enough to open an investigation."

"How is that possible?" she demanded. "He still doesn't believe Jack Marshall is guilty?"

"He doesn't want to. I do think he's having doubts, though. But right now all we have is a missing woman who Marshall has denied having an affair with and an eyewitness to a murder, but no body, no evidence, and Marshall still with a pretty good alibi and a reputation as an upstanding local citizen."

Still she heard something in his voice. "But there's more, isn't there?"

"He suspended me."

"It's all my fault," she cried, and found herself voicing what had been bothering her all morning. "I already feel responsible for Robert Baker getting killed, too. If I hadn't followed Liz to the house and told her everything—"

"Amy Sue, you can't blame yourself for Robert's bad

decisions, and you certainly aren't responsible for me getting suspended. I investigated because it's my job."

"But you did it because you believed that I saw a murder."

"You *did* see a murder. Everything I've learned since has convinced me of that. You saw Jack Marshall kill Whitney Clark."

They both fell silent for a few moments. "Are you giving up, Russ?"

"No," he said slowly. "But I need to go up to the ranch. I usually go on my days off."

"But lately you've been working instead," she said, knowing that it was no longer just about doing his job as a detective. While he wanted justice, he wanted to see this through because of her.

"I was thinking you might want to come with me."

The invitation didn't take her completely by surprise. But what really surprised her was how badly she wanted to go. After everything that had happened, she wouldn't mind taking a step back for a couple of days.

That, however, wasn't the real reason her pulse had taken off at his invite. She wanted to spend more time with him in his other element, the cowboy part of the cop. She also wanted to see where these sparks between them might lead.

"It would just be Saturday night and come back Sunday," he was saying. "You'd have your own room. My parents and brother are there."

She smiled to herself. Russ, the perfect cowboy cop gentleman. "I'd like that." She heard his relief.

"I know they'd like to meet you."

Amy Sue felt her eyebrows shoot up. "Have you told them about me?"

"I never talk about my cases with them, but I might have mentioned you." He sounded shy and maybe a little embarrassed. "How about I pick you up at your hotel in an hour? Will that work?"

"I'll be ready," she said, and felt a shiver of excitement at the thought of an entire weekend with him. She'd barely disconnected when her cell phone rang.

Even before she answered, she'd feared something bad had happened when she saw who was calling. "Liz?"

"I can't do it," the redhead said without preamble. "I've tried. I thought I could let him get away with it after I took his money."

"Took his money? Marshall's money?"

Liz continued as if she hadn't spoken. "I'm just so angry every time I think about him getting away with murdering Whitney, not to mention Robert, because you know it was him."

"Wait, you took his money?" She listened as Liz told her what she'd done, blackmailing him into giving her fifty thousand dollars.

"He paid, didn't even put up a fight. I guess that shows how little fifty grand means to a man like him."

"Great, except he seems more like the kind of man who will get even with you for it. Liz—"

"It just proves that he's guilty."

"You do know that blackmail is against the law, right?" As shocked as she was by what Liz had done, Amy Sue had to agree about the guilty part. But the woman had stepped over a line she shouldn't have crossed. Marshall wouldn't take this lying down, she was sure of that.

"You know he's not going to confess no matter what we do," Liz was saying. "I've decided I'm going to tell his wife. She's the only way to get any justice for Whitney."

"I hate for you to get your hopes up. I had considered doing that, but Liz, what if she already knows?"

"But what matters is that he doesn't believe she knows," Liz said. "He forked over 50K without a fight so I wouldn't tell his wife everything."

It was a strange kind of reasoning. Amy Sue felt sick to her stomach. She was even more worried about Liz after hearing this. "This could get you killed, Liz."

"You said yourself he can't afford anymore dead bodies. I thought you might want to come with me."

She thought of Russ and the trip to the ranch and how badly she wanted it, needed it. "I still think this is a terrible idea, but if I can't talk you out of it—"

"You can't," Liz said emphatically.

"Then I can't let you go alone." She told herself that this wouldn't take long. Christine might not even be home. She probably wouldn't let them into the house. Even if she did and they had their say, the woman would either throw them out or call the cops. Fifteen to twenty minutes tops, she told herself.

As soon as she disconnected, she called Russ. She knew he would try to talk her out of it, but she wanted someone to know where they were going in case there was trouble.

"Bad idea," he said the moment he heard Liz's plan. "Let's not forget that she gave him an alibi for when Liz's husband was killed."

"I know, but I can't let Liz go alone."

"I'll come with you," Russ said.

"A worse idea all things considered," she told him. "You know she won't talk freely with you there. Liz is going to go no matter what I do, and I don't think it will take long."

"How do you know Marshall won't be there or show up?"

She didn't. "Christine might not even be home," she said. "I'll call you as soon as we're done."

"I'm going to wait for you down the street," Russ said. "Things go south I can be there within a few minutes. Call me before you go into the house and keep me connected so I can hear what's being said."

His worry made hers increase. "I'm meeting Liz at the house now."

JACK FELT AS if the storm had passed and he could breathe again. Nothing had come of Detective Russell Tate's visit to his house. Jack was still married, still had his business, still was a free man. Milt must have taken care of it, or the cops didn't have any evidence and couldn't tie him to Robert Baker, let alone Whitney Clark.

He was in the clear, and it felt good. For a while, he'd worried that this was never going to blow over. He'd panicked when there was no need. He was out fifty thousand dollars, but that was peanuts in the grand scheme of things. It irked him that he'd let her blackmail him, but he'd run out of alternatives. He wouldn't always be in such a tight position. Once he knew he was safe and enough time had passed, he would take care of Liz.

His only concern was his wife. Christine had already been worried about him before the detective had shown up to bust his chops. If she confronted him when he went home tonight, he'd deny everything. He couldn't ever let her know about any of this, or he feared he would lose her.

She wasn't at the dealership. Liz had been bluffing. He ground his teeth, thinking about what he'd do to her one day soon.

But he was more worried about keeping his wife. He'd already decided that he would change. No more women on the side. It wouldn't be easy, but it was for the best. At least for a while. He'd be the perfect husband. He'd take an interest in the remodeling Christine was doing, even that ridiculous "safe room" she was having installed off the living room. He'd even go home at a decent time each night—not even working late.

When his cell rang, he thought it might be his wife. He braced himself but was surprised to see the call was from the chief of police. "Milt? What can I do for you?" he said cheerfully, promising himself that he'd make it up to the man big-time when this was over.

"I just wanted to give you a heads-up," the chief said.

Something in the man's tone warned him. "Why, what's up?" he asked, his good mood dissipating like smoke. His heart was already pounding so hard he thought he might have an anxiety attack.

"That detective, Tate, I don't think he's going to stop. I suspended him, but he's compiled quite a lot of information about you and the night of the murder. It's all circumstantial at this point, but…it doesn't look good, Jack. Is there anything you want to tell me? You know I'll try to protect you as much as I can but—"

"There's nothing to tell, Milt. All this is ridiculous.

It will blow over. Like you said, it's all circumstantial. You know me."

"Yeah," the chief agreed. "It seems pretty ridiculous to me, but—"

"It is ridiculous. Don't worry about it. I'm certainly not. I appreciate you calling, though. You have always looked out for me and my business. You're a good friend. I'll make it up to you this summer in my new boat up at Fort Peck Lake. We just need to catch some really big walleyes and laugh about all of this."

"Sure," Milt said, but not sounding all that enthusiastic.

"Thanks again for calling." He disconnected and put down his phone on his desk, his hand shaking. Had some new information come to light? Or was it just everything piling up, since between Detective Tate and Amy Sue Brand, the cops now had the name of the missing—and possibly murdered—woman.

He rued the day he'd seen Whitney standing beside the road with her thumb out. If he hadn't stopped… He put his head into his hands and tried to assure himself that he would get through this.

When his cell rang yet again, he jumped, half afraid it was Milt calling back to say cops were on their way to arrest him. It was a relief to see that it was Christine. He hesitated, not wanting to talk to her right now. He was still upset after Milt's call.

But she seldom called him at work, so he knew it must be important. He picked up.

Chapter Twenty-Three

"She might not be home," Amy Sue said as she and Liz looked up at the house after parking their cars in the huge driveway out front. The garage doors were all closed. No way of knowing if there were cars inside.

"I called to tell her I was coming over right after I talked to you," Liz said. "She's home."

"You did?" Amy Sue hated to think what they might be walking into. "You told her why we wanted to see her?"

"Of course not. I did say it was about her husband and it was important, that's all," Liz said.

That should be more than enough for starters, Amy Sue thought. "Okay, we tell her what we know and then we get out of there, right?" Liz grunted in response. "We let her decide what to do with the information."

"Sure," Liz said.

Amy Sue felt the reassuring weight of her phone in her pocket. Before she'd exited her SUV, she'd called Russ. He had told her not to check the phone, let alone disconnect the call. She had to assume he was still there. His concern had seemed unwarranted. Yet as she and Liz walked to the front door and rang the bell she found comfort in knowing he was somewhere close by and hopefully still listening.

Christine opened the door elegantly dressed, definitely overdressed for this meeting. She looked relaxed, maybe a little curious, possibly even amused as she let the two of them into her gorgeous house.

"We can talk in here," she said as they followed her deeper into the house. "Please excuse the mess. We're remodeling." Amy Sue noticed a large steel door that had been added in one of the walls. Christine must have seen her staring at her. "That will be hidden once the safe room is finished. May I offer you something to drink?"

Amy Sue was wondering why they would be adding a safe room off the living room when Liz asked, "Do you have vodka?" She shot her a warning look. The last thing she needed was for Liz to get drunk.

"Just kidding, kinda," Liz mumbled. "Like I said on the phone—"

"Wouldn't you like to sit first?" Christine asked, definitely amused now.

Amy Sue wondered if Jack Marshall's mistresses had paid her visits and she'd heard it all before. Well, maybe not heard it all, she amended.

"We won't be staying that long," Amy Sue said.

At the same time, Liz said, "Sure, why not" and plopped down in an offered chair. "Let's get right to it. Your husband is a cheater and a killer. He murdered my friend after he'd been seeing her for months, after he'd promised to divorce you and marry her. He even took her to a house under construction to show it to her, letting her think he was buying it for the two of them. That's where he killed her."

Amy Sue had been watching Christine for a reaction to Liz laying it out the way she had. Her eyes had widened, but only slightly. Other than that, there was no reaction or response. Unlike Liz, the two of them were still standing. It looked as if this was going to be over even quicker than Amy Sue had thought.

"I know this sounds unbelievable," Amy Sue said, filling the silence that followed. "But I saw it happen and recognized your husband."

"She was an eyewitness to the murder," Liz interjected.

"Later I found out the woman's name, Whitney Clark. While her body hasn't been found, she's been missing since that night."

"I see," Christine said, frowning. "Did you go to the police?"

"Of course, she did," Liz snapped. "But your husband has the cops in his pocket. We thought you should know what kind of man you're married to. He killed my ex-husband up on the rims."

Amy Sue saw something change in Christine's face. It was subtle, but still she realized that Liz had finally hit a nerve.

"Robert was a fool for trying to blackmail him, but you should know, your husband also gave me fifty grand to keep me quiet."

"Except you didn't stay quiet, did you?" Christine said.

Both Amy Sue and Liz were now staring at the woman.

"You knew," Amy Sue said under her breath.

"Seriously?" Liz demanded. "You know you're married to a murderer?"

"It seems pretty clear, Liz, that she's okay with it," Amy Sue said, feeling a new kind of tension in the dense air around them. "We should go."

Christine sighed and said conversationally, "Don't you realize how dangerous it was for you two to come here? As you pointed out, my husband is a murderer. He's also a psychopath. You must have realized that if you didn't stop trying to get him arrested, he would kill you as well and get away with it."

"If you know this about him, then why haven't you gone to the police?" Amy Sue demanded. She thought she heard the sound of a vehicle, then the slamming of a car door outside and breathed in relief. Russ must not have been far away.

"Because it would be my word against his."

"You're his wife, if you told the police what you know—"

"If there was even a remote chance I had evidence against him I would be dead. No, he'd never make that mistake. By now haven't you realized how good he is at this? He doesn't make mistakes."

"But he did. I witnessed the murder. I saw him!"

She shook her head. "Still, he isn't behind bars, is he? And he won't be even when he kills you both."

"How can you stay with a…murderer?" Liz demanded.

Christine's laugh was brittle. "I had no illusions when I married him. I saw potential in him and the life he could offer me. I didn't care about his affairs with other women.

Marriage is a bargaining chip. I got what I wanted, he got what he wanted."

"You couldn't have known who you were marrying," Amy Sue argued, listening for Russ. Maybe he was having trouble getting into the house.

"I got more than I bargained for," Christine said, and touched the diamond bracelet at her wrist. "Nor do I ever want to have this conversation again. You've put me in danger as well as yourselves." Her voice cracked as she looked toward the front entrance to the house where they'd come in.

"That's Jack," Christine cried. "He can't find you here. Please, hurry. There isn't time. Quick, get inside the safe room," she said, moving quickly to open the door. "I'll get rid of him."

Liz had risen from the chair and was already heading for the safe room. Amy Sue hadn't moved, but the urgency in Christine's voice made her follow Liz.

The moment they stepped in, the door closed with a clunk behind them. Amy Sue heard it lock. Liz must have, too, because she stepped to the door and tried to open it.

"She locked us in," Liz said, something sounding a lot like fear in her voice. "You don't think…" Their gazes met. "I have a bad feeling about this."

Amy Sue couldn't have agreed more as she looked around the small room. It was still under construction, so it was completely empty, the floor as bare as the walls. All she could hope was that Russ was still on the call in her pocket as she dug out her phone.

Her heart dropped as she heard nothing on the other end. When she tried to call him back, she found there was no cell service in here. All she could hope was that he'd heard what was going on before they were disconnected.

Liz had gone to the door and now pressed one ear against it.

"Can you hear anything?"

"Nothing." She turned to face Amy Sue. "What do you think is going on out there?"

She had to swallow before she said, "I have no idea." She didn't say what she was thinking. Christine had known about her husband and now she'd locked them in this room. From the thickness of the walls, Amy Sue doubted anyone would hear them even if they screamed, and there was nothing to use to try to break out.

"Our cars are parked out front," Liz said as if she'd been thinking what Amy Sue had. "She can't keep us in here." She looked toward the ceiling. "Shouldn't there be air vents?"

Chapter Twenty-Four

Josie felt the ominous darkness approaching as if it were sneaking in on the breeze. She rubbed her temples. It had been so long since she could sense trouble that she didn't trust it at first. All her life she'd sensed when something dangerous was coming. It usually came as a darkness on the horizon growing ever closer, ever darker. She never knew what it was exactly, just that it involved someone she knew, someone she cared about.

Her grandmother had second sight or the "knowing" as she often referred to it. She thought it a gift. Josie didn't have it as strongly as her gram. Also, for her, she'd always thought of it more as a curse rather than a gift. She'd told herself that she didn't want to see something awful coming.

But after her accident last year, she'd lost her ability to sense anything in the future. At first she'd been thankful. Now that it seemed to be returning and she feared it had to do with her sister, she did as her grandmother used to encourage her to do. She embraced it, closing her eyes and willing herself to really see for the first time.

All she knew was that Amy Sue was in trouble, just as she'd feared would happen when her sister had been determined to see a killer brought to justice.

Josie opened her eyes. The darkness she'd seen earlier creeping in from the horizon was now black. As it moved toward her she stared inwardly, reaching into that menacing mist, afraid yet knowing she had to see what she'd feared most.

Her sister was in trouble.

JACK DIDN'T KNOW what to expect after getting his wife's cryptic phone call.

"I need you home right now." That's all she'd said before she disconnected. He told himself that if she was in real trouble she would have called 911—not him. But he kept thinking about this morning when Detective Tate had come to the house and Christine had repeated what he told her about the night before.

She'd known he was lying. He'd seen in it her face. Yet she'd lied to Tate for him. At the time, he knew it was going to cost him. Fortunately, he'd already decided to change. Did this rather frantic-sounding call have something to do with the lie?

It wasn't until he pulled in the drive that he saw the two cars parked in front of his house. He recognized them both. Amy Sue Brand's SUV and Liz Baker's older-model car that had seen better days.

He glanced toward the house feeling his temper rise. What were those two women doing here? It didn't take a genius to figure it out, he thought as he parked his car in the garage and got out. They'd come to tell his wife.

Jack swore, thinking of the fifty thousand dollars he'd paid Liz to keep her mouth shut. She would pay for this. Hell, so would the alleged eyewitness to his bad deed. He told himself that if he survived this, he and Christine would go on a long cruise. She could invite all the friends she wanted. He just planned to drink and stare out at the ocean.

After what was going on in the house would Christine be going anywhere with him? Doubtful.

He started to push open the door into the house when he heard a noise behind him as the garage door was lifted just enough for someone to sneak under it.

Russ HAD HEARD enough of the conversation among Amy Sue, Liz and Christine long before the connection had ended. He wasn't sure what the women had hoped to get from Jack Marshall's wife. What they'd gotten was confirmation that she knew of her husband's crimes and was too afraid of him to go to the police.

When he saw Jack drive by on his way home this early, Russ knew it was time to end this before someone got killed. He drove his pickup on up to the house, parking next to Amy Sue's SUV. He felt naked without a gun and badge, but told himself with luck he wouldn't need them.

Jack, he realized, must have parked in one of the garage stalls because his big dark ride wasn't parked out front. At the entrance, Russ rang the bell. Nothing happened. He knocked, again no answer, nothing. He could hear no sound inside the house. He tried the door and realized quickly that getting inside would be next to impossible. The place was like a fortress. He pulled out his phone and tried calling Amy Sue back. It went straight to voicemail.

He was questioning calling the cops when he decided to try the garage doors. Only three of the garage doors had vehicles in them, and all the doors were locked except the one Jack had just entered.

Russ lifted it just enough to slip into the cool darkness inside. He could hear the tick, tick, tick of the engine inside the car Jack had driven here as he moved toward the door into the house.

He hadn't gone but a few feet when he heard the sound of a shoe sole scrape on the concrete floor. He started to turn, the hair at his neck prickling an instant before something hard slammed into his head. As he fell against one of the cars, he heard Jack Marshall let out an oath that ended with "damned cowboy detective" just before Marshall blindsided him with another blow. This one sent him to the concrete floor and the darkness waiting for him.

Chapter Twenty-Five

Jack stood for a moment looking down at the lawman lying on his garage floor. He looked dead. Staggering back, he was already coming up with the story he would tell the cops. The man had broken into his house.

But as he did, he realized that wasn't what really had him worried. He had no idea what was going on upstairs inside the house with his wife and the two women he knew were in there with her. Somehow, that felt more dangerous.

Bracing himself, he entered the house and took the expensive but wonderfully silent elevator to the main floor. He'd loved this house from the first moment he saw it. The view was incredible. From his bedroom window on the fourth floor, he could see his city, Billings, the largest city in Montana and where he'd made his mark.

Christine had argued the house was too large, too ostentatious, too expensive for where they were in life. He hadn't made his fortune yet when he'd purchased the house with all its bedrooms and baths. He'd planned to fill it with his sons who would take over the business and daughters he would one day walk down the aisle with. He had plans that his sons would take over what he'd built and make the family even more prominent and wealthy.

But he'd soon learned that he was unable to have children. It had been a heartbreaking blow to his ego. That was when he really started running around with other women. From the outside it might have looked as if he had something to prove; he didn't care. Christine had mentioned adopting, but he only wanted children from his own seed.

The elevator door opened on the living room and kitchen level. He peered out, surprised to see no one, not even his wife.

"Christine?" Stepping out of the elevator, he called again a little louder.

"Jack."

The sound of her voice directly behind him made him jump. He spun around to see her come out of the kitchen, which in itself was odd. Christine didn't cook. Jack wondered why they even had a kitchen except for the wine fridge.

Standing backlit in a shaft of sunlight shooting through all those magnificent windows he loved, her face was in shadow. But while he couldn't see her expression, the light did catch on her slim wrist and the beautiful, very expensive tennis bracelet he'd bought her. One of many "guilt" presents he'd given her. Only the best for his wife.

"Christine?" His voice cracked as he raised his gaze to watch her stop just inches from him. Her expression was one of calm concern. He cleared his throat. "What's going on?"

"There's something you need to take care of, Jack." Her tone was as calm as her expression. "In the safe room."

He glanced over at the closed steel door of the room Christine had insisted they needed to add during this latest remodel. "What's in there?" His voice came out a whisper. What he meant to ask, he realized, was the question that he'd had since her call. "*Who's* in there?"

She didn't answer, but then she didn't have to. He knew.

"You can fix this, Jack."

He shook his head. He couldn't imagine how. He wouldn't even know where to begin, because he'd lost control of the entire situation. And now there were two women locked in the safe room to deal with, not to mention that body out in the garage.

"It's over," but as he said it, he fought the idea of giving up like a man determined to get out of the desert alive against all odds. There had to be a way out of this. He just hadn't thought of it yet.

"You have to fix this." Christine's voice held none of the panic now hammering away in his chest making it hard to breathe. "You made this mess." She made it sound as if he'd tracked in mud—not this catastrophe he'd brought home.

He met her gaze, his beautiful perfect wife, the symbol of the perfect life he'd built with her help. His ice princess. He wasn't even that shocked that she'd always known what kind of man he really was and had looked the other way.

Even with two women locked in their safe room, she was calmer than what he thought was normal. He'd worked so hard for so long to prove that he was worthy of a woman like Christine and the life that came with her.

Yet she wasn't what he'd wanted or needed when he

wasn't being the Jack Marshall everyone thought he was. Like this house, she'd been for show, he realized with a flash of insight.

And now here they were. He couldn't imagine how things could get worse until she moved to him and pressed something into his hand before stepping back.

He looked down to find the knife handle in his palm and felt a shock. It looked exactly like the knife he'd taken from the kitchen to kill Whitney. He liked to believe he was only going to threaten her with the knife, but he'd known the only way to be rid of her was to kill her. He'd planned to replace the knife before Christine knew it had gone missing, but when things had gone south, he'd forgotten. Apparently, she paid more attention to the kitchen than he thought, because this was identical to the one he'd thrown away—except for the lack of blood.

Jack shook his head slowly, thinking of what could be waiting for him behind the steel door. He already had the detective lying dead in the garage. He hadn't meant to kill him, but the cop had been a pain in his backside for weeks and then to see him breaking into his house…

"I can't," he whispered. He was so tired. He just wanted to go back to that day on the interstate when he spotted the young woman hitching a ride. He would sell his soul to change it all.

But when he looked into his wife's eyes, he knew he'd sold his soul a long time ago, and the day of reckoning had arrived.

"This is your mess, Jack," she said, and turned to walk back toward the kitchen.

His fingers closed around the handle of the knife against his will.

Amy Sue looked over at Liz sitting on the floor of the small unfinished room. There'd been that moment of panic for both of them when they'd realized there were no air vents yet in the room.

She'd had to talk Liz into sitting and calming down. "If there isn't enough air, then we need to conserve it. Panicking isn't going to help. Just the opposite."

"I can't believe this was my stupid idea," Liz said now. She'd been quiet, no doubt ruminating as Amy Sue had been doing. Both of them regretted that they'd put themselves in this position as they waited, afraid of what was going to happen next. As if being locked in this airless room wasn't enough. "I was so sure that if his wife knew, she'd call the cops and this would be over."

Amy Sue nodded, but said nothing. *Would'ves and should'ves*, her Gram would have said. *Thinkin' to change the past is a fool's errand. Only thing you can change is yourself in the future.*

"What do you think they're going to do with us?" Liz asked quietly.

Wasn't like anyone outside this room could hear them. The walls were thick with soundproof material. It made Amy Sue wonder what the real purpose of this room was. Maybe exactly what it was being used for now. It scared her to think that other women had shown up here to confront Christine hoping she would do something about her husband.

"If Christine wanted to kill us, she would have already." It was the only positive answer Amy Sue had.

"But now Jack Marshall is out there," Liz pointed out.

Amy Sue realized that neither of them had actually seen him or even really heard him come into the house before Christine had ushered them into this room. Maybe he wasn't out there. Maybe he had no idea how far his wife would go—

Before she could finish her thought, she heard the steel door lock click. The door swung open. Jack Marshall filled the doorway.

Seeing Jack standing there, his expression dark and unreadable, was terrifying, but nothing like the knife he had clutched in his hand.

Chapter Twenty-Six

Russ woke on the hard concrete floor. His head throbbed and blood ran down in one eye. He wiped at it as he struggled to get to his feet. On the floor next to him lay the tire iron with more of his blood on it. He picked it up, feeling a little dizzy but more focused than when he'd first regained consciousness.

Jack Marshall had left him for dead. The man just kept making mistakes, he told himself as he headed for the door that he knew must lead into the house. He wished he had his gun, but the tire iron would have to do, he thought as he considered taking the elevator, then chose the stairs.

He didn't know how long he'd been out. Not long from what he could tell. He had no way of knowing what floor of the four-story house he'd find Jack on—let alone Amy Sue and Liz. From what he'd heard on the phone before they'd been disconnected, both women were in serious danger.

Climbing the stairs quickly, he tried not to think the worst, but it was hard knowing what Jack Marshall would do. Then again, he knew firsthand what the man was capable of, Russ thought, as he put his hand to his throbbing head. Fortunately, the bleeding hadn't been extensive and had now mostly quit.

Quickly stopping at each floor along the stairs to listen, he moved upward until he heard voices on the third floor and eased open the door to step out. He sucked in a lungful of relief at the sound of Amy Sue's voice even though he couldn't make out her words.

Moving toward the voices, he stayed out of sight. As he slipped behind a large cabinet, he peered around it into the massive living room. From what he could see, it appeared that the Marshalls were in the process of remodeling. They had changed one of the walls to make what looked like a small room between the living area and the also massive kitchen.

His heart began to pound harder as he realized that's where Amy Sue's voice was coming from.

Amy Sue was on her feet at the sight of Jack standing in the doorway with a large lethal-looking knife. "You don't want to do this. Detective Tate is—"

"Dead," Jack said. "He can't help you."

The shock of his words hit her. "You bastard," she said, her voice breaking with grief. It was all she could do not to launch herself at the man, knife or no knife. Good sense kept her where she was as her hands balled into fists. Russ gone? Her heart instantly filled with a drowning sorrow for what could have been, followed by a wave of guilt. She had gotten him to this house. Why hadn't she gone with him to the ranch. But even as she thought it, she knew she couldn't have let Liz come here alone. Just as she hadn't been able to let Jack Marshall get away with murder. "You're a monster."

He looked hurt. "You know nothing about me."

"I know you're a murderer," Amy Sue snapped. "But

if you kill the two of us, too, the police aren't going to protect you anymore. You're going to kill us with a knife? Whitney was killed with a knife. You don't think they'll put that together? People know that we came here, my sister for one," she bluffed. "If she doesn't hear from me soon, she'll have the cops beating down your doors."

"She's right," Liz said, hope in her voice. "I told a friend of mine from work that if I didn't show up for my shift to call the cops. I gave her your address."

Jack shook his head. "You've left me no choice," he said but didn't move. "I tried to warn you. If you'd just let it go and minded your own business."

"Jack, just finish it," Christine said from behind him.

Amy Sue hadn't noticed her. As she did she felt a shock rattle through her. The woman was telling him to kill them. But what was more shocking was the gun she had pointed at Jack's head.

Russ only had a few seconds to assess the situation and act. He was literally outgunned with both Christine and Jack armed with weapons, while he only had a tire iron. But he did have the element of surprise since he'd just heard Jack tell Amy Sue that he was dead.

As he moved quietly across the thick living room carpet, he couldn't believe what he was seeing. Jack Marshall had a knife and Christine was egging her husband on. More astonishing was that it appeared she would shoot him if he didn't kill the two women.

Or did she plan on shooting him *after* he killed Amy Sue and Liz? She could say she tried to stop him, that she had no idea he'd killed some woman he'd been cheating on her with, that she hadn't known.

Russ tucked the tire iron in his jeans, freeing both hands as he reached her. He went for the gun as he cupped his hand over her mouth and dragged her back out of sight of the room's doorway.

She was stronger than she looked, putting up more of a struggle than he expected. If not for his head injuries he could still have taken her down easily. He wrestled the gun from her, but she kept fighting using self-defense training as she attacked him.

Russ had hoped to do this quickly and quietly, but Christine Marshall wasn't having any of that. As he grabbed her to take her down, she threw them both off-balance. They went down hard, Christine hitting her head on the edge of the glass coffee table and Russ slamming into the floor hard.

AMY SUE HAD seen Christine suddenly disappear from behind Jack as she was grabbed from behind. She had no idea what was going on. At the sounds behind him, Jack turned, giving her the opportunity she'd been waiting for.

She jumped on his back, slamming her fist into his neck and making him howl. Shocked, she saw that Russ was trying to subdue Christine, who was fighting him with everything she had. The gun she'd been holding on Jack just minutes ago was on the floor some distance away.

"Liz, get the gun!" she cried as Jack tried to throw her off. She kept punching him, going for his face when he tried to turn around. He still had the knife in his hand as Liz rushed past him into the living room.

It happened quickly and yet for Amy Sue, the battle had gone on forever. With her legs wrapped around him, she'd managed to hit Jack in the face, holding on to his hair to keep him from throwing her off as she pummeled him with her free fist until her hand was slick with blood from his bleeding nose.

They all started at the loud crack when Christine's head hit the edge of the glass coffee table. In what had looked like slow motion, Liz had the gun and had pointed it Jack but hadn't taken a shot because she feared she would kill Amy Sue.

Russ lay on the floor seeming momentarily stunned, Christine lying next to him, her head bleeding profusely, as the sound of sirens filled the air.

"Drop the knife, Jack," the suspended detective said as he got to his feet. He moved to Liz and had to wrestle the gun from her hands.

"You know he'll get off if we let him go," Liz argued as Russ peeled her fingers from the weapon and turned it on Jack.

"Drop the knife," he repeated. Amy Sue was still on the man's back, one hand buried in his hair. "Liz, go down and open the front door for the cops."

It wasn't until Liz moved that Amy Sue felt Jack give up.

The knife clattered to the floor. Jack seemed to see his wife bleeding on the carpet and moved like a sleep-walker toward her as the cops rushed in.

By then, Russ had put down the gun and reached for Amy Sue. She stumbled to him, letting him take her in his arms, holding on as if afraid she could no longer trust gravity and he was the only thing keeping her from fall-ing off the earth.

Chapter Twenty-Seven

Back in that large room at the police department, Amy Sue worried that she wouldn't be believed again. But this time it wasn't Detective Hanson questioning her. The interim chief of police, an older man with graying hair named John Harper, did the questioning. He'd been brought in when Russ had filed a formal complaint against the chief and Detective Hanson for trying to keep evidence from coming out about Jack Marshall.

Amy Sue had already given her statement, but had been told that the new interim chief had a few questions. She wanted to hear that Jack had confessed to all of it, but knew that was too much to hope for.

"You're the eyewitness," Chief Harper said, nodding. "I've read your statement. I commend you on your bravery and dogged determination to bring Jack Marshall to justice."

"Actually, my sister Josie was right. I had no business doing it," she said. "He was just so sure he could get away with murder. I knew he'd do it again, and I didn't want that to happen."

Harper smiled. "While I appreciate your efforts, I hope your sleuthing days are over."

"They are. Were you able to find Whitney Clark?"

He nodded. "Detective Russell Tate told us where he suspected she'd been buried."

"At the construction site where she was killed," Amy Sue said, and he nodded. He didn't say that she should have been found a lot sooner if Detective Tate had been given the authority to investigate like he'd wanted to.

But they both must have been thinking about that because Harper said, "Detective Tate has been reinstated and given a commendation. I was sorry that he's resigned from the department. The door is always open for a man like him should he want to come back." Amy Sue didn't see that happening, but she kept it to herself. As Russ said, he was a cowboy through and through. It's one of the reasons she'd fallen in love with him. "I suppose you know he's being released from the hospital today."

"I'm picking him up this afternoon," she said. "He saved my life."

"From what you told us, he saved all of your lives."

She had to ask. "Did Jack confess?"

"He's talking," the chief said.

"What about his wife Christine?"

"She's come out of surgery. The doctor said she'll survive, but no charges are being brought against her." Amy Sue started to speak but he held up a hand. "We can't arrest someone for what they might have been planning to do. She swears she put the two of you into the safe room to protect you from Jack."

Shaking her head, Amy Sue said, "She told him to kill us, then she was going to kill him to save herself, but no, I have no proof that was her intent. I only know what I saw in her face before Russ took the gun away from her. She'd put up with Jack's philandering for years to protect the privileged life she was living. She would have done anything not to lose it."

"I can't promise that she won't lose it. More than likely society will feel sorry for her, the naive wife who had no idea what her husband was doing—or had done. You might not have gotten all the justice you wanted, but you got a murderer off the street," Harper said as he rose. "Let that be enough."

Amy Sue might have argued that it wasn't enough, but she was more than willing to put it all behind her. A certain former cowboy detective had promised her a date. She stood to leave, anxious to get to the hospital to pick up Russ. They were going to his family ranch while he recuperated, then she was taking him home with her to Dry Gulch.

She didn't have her sister Josie's second sight, but the way she saw it, the future looked bright and sunny.

Sitting in Goldie's diner in the heart of Dry Gulch, Montana, Russ couldn't take his eyes off his date. He'd promised Amy Sue a real date, once he recovered from his injuries. They'd spent some time at his family ranch. He hadn't been surprised that his mother and father and brother had fallen for Amy Sue like he had. She was right at home in the kitchen with his mother as well as out doing chores with him and his brother.

"If you could go to any restaurant anywhere in the world, where would you like our first date to be?" he'd asked after they'd gone to her family ranch. He already knew her sister Josie and liked her. Russ was a little surprised, though, how easily Josie had accepted the fact that he and Amy Sue were now a couple—and they hadn't been on one official date yet.

"Anywhere in the world, no matter what I want to eat?" Amy Sue had asked, then grinned. "I pick Goldie's in Dry Gulch."

He'd laughed, not surprised. He'd come to know this woman and what she wanted from life. He'd felt a closeness to her from the beginning. She was smart, determined, beautiful and even more stubborn than he was, and he'd fallen madly in love with her.

Goldie, the diner owner and Josie's best friend and sister-in-law, took their orders. The daily special, which today just happened to be meat loaf, mashed potatoes and green beans with iced tea and a piece of Goldie's famous chocolate cake for dessert.

Russ felt as if he'd found a second family in the small quaint diner.

"Goldie and Josie just told me that they are both pregnant. Their babies are due around the same time," Amy Sue said, and grinned. "I can't wait to be an aunt."

He'd been carrying his grandmother's ring around in his pocket since he'd gotten it from his mother. "You'll be the best mother, too." He slid out of the booth and dropped to one knee. "Marry me, Amy Sue Brand."

Tears flooded her eyes, then she laughed. "What will our children say when I tell them you asked me to marry you on our very first date, Russell Tate?"

"They'll say it was clearly meant to be. Was that yes?"

She slid from the booth and into the cowboy's arms as he put the engagement ring on her finger and kissed her.

"Best date ever," she said as everyone in the diner

clapped and cheered, including her sister, Josie, whom Goldie had called so she didn't miss this.

"Welcome to Dry Gulch," Amy Sue joked.

He met her gaze and held it. "Feels like home to me," he said, and kissed her again.

* * * * *

Get up to 4 Free Books!

We'll send you 2 free books from each series you try
PLUS a free Mystery Gift.

Both the **Harlequin Intrigue®** and **Harlequin® Romantic Suspense** series feature compelling novels filled with heart-racing action-packed romance that will keep you on the edge of your seat.

YES! Please send me 2 FREE novels from the Harlequin Intrigue or Harlequin Romantic Suspense series and my FREE gift (gift is worth about $10 retail). I may cancel anytime by emailing ReaderServiceInfo@Harlequin.com or by calling 1-800-873-8635. If I don't cancel, I will receive 6 brand-new Harlequin Intrigue Larger-Print books every month and be billed just $7.19 each in the U.S. or $7.99 each in Canada, or 4 brand-new Harlequin Romantic Suspense books every month and be billed just $6.39 each in the U.S. or $7.19 each in Canada, a savings of 20% off the cover price. It's quite a bargain! Shipping and handling is just 75¢ per book in the U.S. and $1.75 per book in Canada.* I understand that accepting the free books and gift places me under no obligation to buy anything—they are mine to keep for free no matter what I decide.

Choose one:
☐ **Harlequin Intrigue Larger-Print** (199/399 BPA G3CD)
☐ **Harlequin Romantic Suspense** (240/340 BPA G3CD)
☐ **Or Try Both!** (199/399 & 240/340 BPA G3CE)

Name (please print)

Address   Apt. #

City   State/Province   Zip/Postal Code

Email: Please check this box ☐ if you would like to receive newsletters and promotional emails from Harlequin Enterprises ULC and its affiliates. You can unsubscribe anytime.

Mail to the **Harlequin Reader Service:**
IN U.S.A.: P.O. Box 1341, Buffalo, NY 14240-8531
IN CANADA: P.O. Box 603, Fort Erie, Ontario L2A 5X3

Want to explore our other series or interested in ebooks? Visit www.ReaderService.com or call 1-800-873-8635.

HIHRS2603